The pastor's wife is murdered; her dog is also killed.

Using a "hair-brained" theory to find a matching dog hair, Sheriff Colton Mitchell follows twists and turns to locate the killer.

OTHER BOOKS BY MARY JANE BRYAN

The Catch of Misee Sue
Spiral
Errant
No Small Deceit
A Morning's Worth of Murder

Murder At Dutch Mills

A Colton Mitchell Mystery

Mary Jane Bryan

A Black Opal Books Publication

Prelude

The figure moved furtively at the edge of the wood, one slow step at a time. It was a shadow within shadows. This person knew that the security light at the top of the small hill had been out for some time. Even when on, the light did not reach the edge of the clearing, which formed an oval pattern from the house to the edge of the undergrowth. There would always be several feet of darkness at night around the clearing, beyond the scope of the light.

This area of darkness was what the person was counting on to give protection as it slinked its way toward the house at the top of the small hill.

There was no moonlight. The moon was in its smallest phase, making only a sliver in the dark sky. Clouds covered that sliver.

It had already started to rain. The forecast had predicted a heavy thunderstorm at this time on this night. The weather was a major factor for the plan this night.

There were to be straight-line winds as well as this storm, a possible tornado even, as a result of a hurricane in the Gulf which was sending this weather clear up into Northwest Arkansas, and then was predicted to "hook" around on itself and return the same way. This was very unusual this far inland.

Presently, it was dumping lots of rain, thunder, and lightning on the whole area.

Beyond the house there was a cemetery. This cemetery was a typical one found in the countryside of Arkansas. There was always a small, usually white-framed country church, then a cemetery beside or behind it to service the various members that passed away through the years. Members may not even be required to buy a plot. Some of the gravestones would show dates as far back as the middle 1800s, or even older.

More and more, people were being buried closer to the bigger cities, but once in a while, these country cemeteries were still used.

There was a house down the lane past the cemetery, but it was located over a knoll and was not visible from this house. Unless a sleepless person was out and about in the middle of the night, this figure would not be seen from there.

The figure was dressed in all black—black the color of mystery, of fear, of death. Black, the color associated with anguish and the unknown. The color black was associated with the feeling of being incognito, able to create an inconspicuous feeling, enabling the wearer to blend into various scenes.

To this person, it was simply a way to stay as inconspicuous as possible, to blend into the shadows and not be seen.

The "man of the house" was gone. The masked person thought of this man as less than being what this term implied, but still this man was absent, gone to a meeting of like-minded people.

This left the wife and small dog at home. The dog was what one thought of as being a "yip-yip" dog. All shrill bark at the top of its lungs and occasionally, maybe, a nip at the ankles in the false hope that a person would feel intimidated at this pretend-type guard dog.

But this meant stealth and slowness were all the more important. Slow motion would win the day. The person smiled. This *night,* slow motion would win the *night.*

Still keeping to the shadows, the figure made its way around the side to the back of the house, to the cemetery side of the property. Inching along the back of the house, it came to the sliding glass doors that went from the dining/kitchen area to the back patio.

Heavy rain was now pouring down. Lightning, then its accompanying thunder, was rapidly drawing closer. The sound of thunder would be an advantage.

The house was built at a time when sliding glass doors were popular. The only difference in this house and the typical ranch style of the time, was the fact that the master bedroom was in the center of the house, at the front, with the door off the dining/kitchen area and not at the end of a hall containing three bedrooms, a hall bath, and a half bath in the master bedroom. Well, maybe a full bath if the owner were lucky.

Still, the figure thought the floor plan was laid out to offer an advantage. Even if the yippy dog started barking, it would only be for a bark or two before it could be silenced. It was the understanding of this person that the wife slept with a "sleep machine" ($50 at Walmart, but you would probably have to order online) going and earplugs.

A conversation overheard had supplied this information.

Good to know.

The wife had commented that although it was so quiet and peaceful in this place, she had grown accustomed to the noise of the machine from when they lived in the married apartments at seminary. The apartment walls were not that well-built. Both people in the conversation had laughed and agreed that nothing was built like it used to be.

Not only would it keep the dog from hearing any sounds too soon, but certainly keep the wife asleep.

The intruder was depending not only the sounds of the machine and the wife blocking out noises with ear plugs, of this place to mask the deed, but the fact that many people still did not lock their doors at night. Whether they just simply forgot to or were so trusting of the place they lived, would be a question for further discussion.

If one were interested in discussing those finer points, of course.

At the glass doors, the figure paused to listen. No sounds. Not even the dog.

Good.

Fingers covered in fine black gloves reached to grip the latch. The latch gave and the door opened without a sound.

Good, again.

The opening only had to be big enough for a body to go in sideways. Opening it enough for a frontal entrance would take too long.

The figure slipped in, still as quiet as a mouse.

No dog.

Could it not be here?

The gun was pointing and ready to silence the dog.

Suddenly, there came the sound of a "flop" onto the floor in the master bedroom and the dog came out.

"Splisht."

There was only one "yip" and maybe not even a full one before there were no more.

Silently, the figure went to the door of the master bedroom.

The person in the bed rose up to see what the matter was. Two bullets in quick succession caused her to fall back on the bed. Thunder masked the sound of the gun.

There was no doubt she was dead. Both bullets had pierced the center of her heart.

The person shooting was a marksman.

Chapter 1

Henry Carlton stepped out on his front porch. He made sure the screen door closed silently. He took a step away from door and leaned his back against the house. The thin, dark green robe he had thrown on over his t-shirt, the one he always slept in, did not keep out the slight chill of this early spring morning.

It was not quite dawn.

Henry and the missus were heading out this morning to visit her sister across the state. They planned on leaving at 4:15 a.m., and it was only 4:00. Might as well let the missus sleep as long as possible. Traveling was getting to be harder and harder on her. If he would admit it, driving the semi-annual trek, maybe a third time, even, to the sister's home was getting harder and harder for him, also. But he would not admit that yet.

The truck was packed, with the suitcases and boxes strapped down in the bed with bungee cords so they were secure. He'd packed the night before. He knew everything would be safe overnight.

Nothing ever happened here.

He had brought his cigarette pack and lighter out with him. A quick smoke would be good right now.

Just then a faint light shone through the small trees and scrub bushes that lined the fence from his front gate to the end of his fence down at the corner. His fence ended where the dirt road in this small community went two ways. The "entrance" to the community, which really could not be called a road because it was so short, turned in off State Highway 59, went across a small bridge over a small creek and a few hundred yards before a person had to turn either right toward a few houses down the way, or left on a dirt road that would go for three miles south before it reached State Highway 244. This three-mile stretch of rocky, dirt road paralleled the Arkansas/Oklahoma state line, allowing for only one house at a time down the road on the west side, with a little property on it before the land belonged to the State of Oklahoma.

He had wondered over the years how many Arkansas as opposed to Oklahoma deer had been killed over the years.

The light was followed quickly by the sound of what he thought was a car door. But the door was not slammed but closed quietly. It probably didn't even latch all the way. But he could not see a car for the foliage along the fence.

He straightened up to get a better look.

Headlights went on but the vehicle did not move. Since the security lights at the corner of these "streets" had burned out when the security light at the parsonage had, he had no way of seeing what kind of vehicle it was. It looked like a small, light-colored car, but he couldn't tell exactly. He didn't see an overhead light come on inside the vehicle. Damn the electric company. He knew several people had called about these lights and they kept saying that were going to repair them, but here they were. Still down.

He didn't blame himself for an overgrown, bushy fence row, making visibility of the vehicle difficult as it continued to sit there. He had commented several times that he needed to clean it out. But you know how that goes.

Then the car started to move slowly, turning the corner toward the highway.

He watched, not being able to see the lights for a few seconds. Another house sat in that short stretch of dirt road, facing north. He thought he saw a flicker of lights among the trees going south on Highway 59 once, but no more, so he assumed the car turned north. Again, there was a healthy stand of trees along the creek that ran parallel to the road, so maybe he just didn't see any lights with this rain.

He shook his head. Teen-agers! Probably just a couple of no-good teen-agers out all night, necking and drinking. Or, drinking and necking, whichever came first.

He shook his head again. He lit his cigarette. By the time he was finished, it would be time to wake the wife, dress quickly and be off. It would take them all day to reach the sister's house.

Usually they stayed about a week, maybe longer, depending on everyone's mood. If they all got along, the stay might extend to two weeks.

At least the fishing was good along the sister's property on the White River.

Chapter 2

When Kelli couldn't get the pastor's wife, Maureen, on the phone the next morning, she thought nothing about it. Maureen would not have been expecting her call. They were to meet that afternoon around 3:00 to go over the music for the next Sunday's morning worship service. Maureen was the choir director and Kelli was the church organist. This Sunday morning, Maureen was going to sing a solo, and Kelli would accompany her on the organ.

Maureen was probably out taking a morning walk with that little dog of hers. She could use the exercise, lose some weight. At least that was Kelli's opinion, which she kept to herself, of course.

Kelli did not particularly like Maureen. She thought she was overbearing, always having to have her way on church committees and in all planning for the church. True, the church was a small country church "on the hill," and maybe did not have the greatest pool of talent for certain activities, but that did not give the pastor's wife the right to think she could control all functions, what was done, when, and who did what.

Kelli needed to change the time they were to meet that afternoon. Her son had called last minute this morning to say that they would be at her home at 4:00 that afternoon to spend a three-day weekend with them. There were two grandchildren involved, so naturally she wanted to be there when they arrived. Maureen would be willing to meet her earlier, she was sure.

The pastor was not scheduled to be home until that evening. He was at the state convention which had lasted all week. It was a once-a-year function, so he did not want to miss any of the sessions. The drive from Little Rock would take about four and a half hours. He, and the two men he was with, would leave there at 5:00 p.m.

Kelli got busy with the breakfast dishes. After the dishes were done, she decided to bake a cake. She forgot to call back to Maureen until about an hour and a half later.

Maureen still did not answer the phone at the parsonage. Kelli tried the church phone, but that went unanswered, also.

Strange, thought Kelli. *I don't know her schedule, of course, but she should be in one place or the other.*

The parsonage was just across the driveway, which was an unpaved country lane, from the church. This lane went on past the church, alongside the cemetery until it ended at the house at the end.

Again, she got busy doing the laundry. She dust mopped her hardwood floors while the washing machine was going.

She was grateful for her hardwood floors. They were the original ones in this one-hundred-year-old house; the house her mother had left to her when she passed away. Kelli and her husband had made the decision to retire from each of their respective professions and move to this farmhouse in the country. Since they were each still working past the required retirement time to receive full retirement pay and also their Social Security, they thought it would be a good idea. Her husband, Frank, decided that tending a small herd of cattle would be a good hobby during his retirement. The farmhouse had more than enough land to support a small herd.

They'd remodeled the house, complete with redoing the original hardwood floors. The house had been well maintained during the years her mother had lived there, so it did not take much to remodel it.

As before, she forgot to call Maureen until long after lunch. She had to admit that she was getting more and more forgetful. One thing she knew, though, was that she still had all her musical ability.

She shook her head as she cleaned the dust mop. Maureen didn't think much of Kelli's musical ability, of course, and did not hesitate to give her opinion. It seems Kelli's timing was off this way or that, or Maureen wanted the piece played slower or faster than it was written. Sometimes she wanted a musical "breath" here or there. It was always something and they would go over and over a piece or part of a piece. A cantata always presented a difficult time. These occurred at Christmas and Easter just like clockwork. Kelli never looked forward to them, but this had been her mother's church and she felt it was now her church, so she would remain faithful.

Her grandfather had been one of the original founders of the church. He was considered a "charter" member. The church had the original paperwork, although many original papers had been abused through the years. Her mother had been responsible for collecting them from different rooms of the church and filing them in a special place, displaying the original charter in a frame and place of honor.

How could she leave this church, the church of her grandparents and parents? She loved the church, just not always what was happening there.

She decided to call the pianist, to tell her she needed to meet earlier and did she know how to get hold of Maureen? Janice didn't know how, other than the same phone numbers Kelli had tried. Since she lived closer to the church, her house being on the highway, she volunteered to go right then to see if she could find Maureen around the church.

Kelli remembered to call her son to tell him she might be gone when the family arrived, but Frank would be there. She explained that she had not been able to reach the pastor's wife to schedule an earlier time for practice.

Janice's knocks on the parsonage front door went unanswered. She stepped to the side, cupped her eyes with her hands and looked through the glass at the side of the door. The glass went from the top of the door to the floor. It was designed so the home owner could see who was at the door before opening it.

She saw nothing amiss in the living room and through to the dining room table. Since the garage door was down, she assumed Maureen must be over at the church. She walked over there. She used her key to go in. She had a key to use whenever she wanted to practice the piano and no one else was there.

She called for Maureen as soon as she was inside. The church was small enough that when it was quiet, as it was right now, anyone would hear a shout no matter where they were in the church.

All was silent. No one answered her call. She returned to her car and went home. She called Kelli as soon as she was in her car. They both agreed just to meet at the regular time.

Maureen would be there by then.

Chapter 3

But she wasn't.

Kelli and Janice went through the selected hymns together. They decided they were okay with everything. Janice listened as Kelli went through Maureen's solo for Sunday. She agreed that Kelli was ready, she was a super accompanist.

Maureen still had not arrived.

"Let's go over to the parsonage. Maybe something has happened to her and she can't get to the phone, or something," said Kelli.

That sounded reasonable. They decided to go around to the back door when their knocks went unanswered at the front. They tried the front door and it was locked.

The back sliding-door was unlocked. The inside of the house was dim as Kelli slid the door open.

She stepped in. She stopped so abruptly that Janice ran into her as she stepped in. They both were so shocked it took several seconds for them to move. They both took a step back at the same time, grabbing for the kitchen counter to steady themselves.

They were looking at the dog lying on the floor, blood all over him.

"What…what could this mean?" Janice asked. She realized she was whispering. It seemed appropriate somehow.

"I have no idea," Kelli answered. "Let's check the rest of the house."

She started to the master bedroom first. Why she went that way, straight ahead, she could not tell later.

Just a hunch.

At the door she stopped, putting both hands to her mouth. She felt like her heart stopped. Blood was all over the bed. She knew the person on the bed was dead. That's why she had not answered the phone or met them at 4:00.

She turned to Janice.

"Call 911," she said. "Hurry."

Janice turned to the phone on the kitchen counter and dialed the number with shaking hands. She wasn't sure she wanted to see what was in the bedroom. She knew it was serious, though.

Kelli turned and guided them both out the back door. They walked around to the side of the house. They waited on the driveway, in front of the garage, for the police or ambulance, whichever came first.

They were the first to discover this tragedy. Kelli was the first to see the body.

The image would stay with her for the rest of her life.

Chapter 4

When Washington County Sheriff Colton Mitchell and his chief deputy, Eric, arrived at the scene, they were met immediately by another deputy. They had been on the opposite side of the county, responding to a B&E. They came as soon as they could, lights flashing and all. The forensics team had been called, as well as the coroner.

"You need to come in through the front door, Chief," Leonard said. They called the Sheriff "chief" although that was not his title. When he came as sheriff almost two years ago, someone had called him that and it had stuck.

"The killer came through the back door, which was unlocked, so we have preserved the crime scene for you to see first, waiting for you to instruct us as to how you want to proceed."

"Is the forensics team here?" Colton asked as they all strode toward the front of the house.

"Yes, all lined up and waiting for you," was the reply.

"Someone had to walk in the bedroom, right?"

"Well, yes, that was me, but only me, and I put on the plastic booties to preserve the integrity of what I could."

All three paused on the front threshold to pull plastic booties over their own boots and latex gloves on both hands. It had stormed during the night. A light rain had continued until a few minutes ago.

Colton and Eric walked in the direction his officer pointed. This was an open living room and dining combination with a sliding glass door going out the back to a concrete patio area. The killer had entered by way of this sliding glass door.

Colton shook his head.

Yes, this was about as country as you could get. A very small community, having seen its population growth a century ago, then families moving out one by one to the larger towns to find jobs to feed their families. This community was practically a ghost town now, with just a few residents.

Maybe they just wanted to continue living here or were simply locked in because of economics. Who knew?

But, still. To leave your doors unlocked at night, even here, was unheard of in this day and age. Simply too many loonies had seen too many home invasion movies. Put a little booze down them or a few drugs, and someone was sure to try something.

Someone had.

They first saw the body of the little dog. It was on its side in a pool of blood. It had been shot. It was a Lhasa Apso, or some similar breed. Maybe a mix. He didn't know his dog breeds that well. There seemed to be so many of them these days.

Leonard stepped aside into the kitchen area and pointed toward an open door leading into a room at the front of the house. This was the master bedroom. It seemed an unusual floor plan to him, but to each his own.

As soon as he stepped through the door, Colton stopped. He really didn't need to go any further. He didn't need to touch the corpse. He would leave that to Roy, the coroner, who should be arriving any minute.

The body was that of an overweight woman in her nightgown. It seemed apparent that the killer had shot the dog first as he came through the back door. Maybe the dog had started barking, maybe just enough to wake the woman.

Whatever, it looked as if she may have risen up in bed, but not to the point of putting her legs over the side, then fallen back on the bed. She still had a startled look on her face. She was shot cleanly in the heart, two shots to the heart. Probably one right after the other.

Two shots.

The first probably killed her, because this was the true aim of a marksman, but the killer had shot off the second round just to be sure. One arm was spread out across the bed and the other, the right arm, hung off the bed over the side.

Blood was spread out all over her chest and had soaked into the blankets and sheets.

Quite a mess.

The coroner would locate the bullets with the autopsy and then forensics could determine the make of the bullet, then the type of gun.

Eric was beside him.

The sheriff pointed to a small machine on the nightstand beside the bed, the side next to the woman.

"That's a sleep machine," Eric said. "My wife uses one, or I guess I should say we use one."

"And what does it do?" Colton asked. He had never seen one before.

"It just makes a sound, sort of like a noisy fan, but it doesn't produce any wind. It blocks out outside noises so a person can sleep better. I suppose light sleepers would use them more than anyone else. My wife's a light sleeper. The latest one we bought a few months ago when the one we had went out, but we had it for fifteen years. They are $49.95 through Walmart online."

"Was it on when Leonard arrived?"

"Yes, he said it was. He turned it off. Didn't touch anything but the little knob on the side that you push to turn it off."

Colton just nodded. That would not hurt anything.

"And look," Eric continued. He pointed to the woman's ear next to them. She had an ear plug in her ear. It would be certain there was one in the other ear, also.

"That's why she didn't hear the killer come in. A person must really have a problem if they have to use a sound machine and ear plugs both. I mean, that goes way beyond being a light sleeper. Maybe Roy can find traces of some sleep aid, some pill, in her system.

"Why would she need to shut out any noise around here? I mean, what noise? Ghosts from the cemetery, or what?"

It seemed so incredulous to him that someone would use all this to block out non-existent noises in such a peaceful country setting.

"Habit, probably. Maybe they moved here from a large city. We'll find out all that, I'm sure. That would explain it. Maybe."

All that and an unlocked back door, thought Colton. *Add to that a terrible thunder and lightning storm during the wee hours before dawn to wipe out any footprints or tire print, any other outside evidence.*

Great. Just great.

"Why?" he continued. "This is the pastor's wife, according to the two ladies who found her. Who kills a pastor's wife? You don't like the pastor or his family, you just quit going to that church and find another. There are plenty around. So, why?"

"That's the obvious question, of course," the deputy began. "When we find that out, we can probably locate the killer in rapid order."

"Where is the husband, the preacher?" he asked.

"According to the ladies, he has been gone all week to Little Rock, to the Baptist Convention there. They have an annual conference. The pastor and two other men went. It seems all the people who attend can vote on policies of all the churches, as a whole denomination, and things like that. I'm not a Baptist myself, so I'm not familiar with all the details, just that they had been gone all week."

"When are they expected home?"

"Again, the ladies said this evening. They would have stayed until 5:00, when the last session ended. It takes about four hours, maybe more, depending on stops, to get from Little Rock to here."

It was 6:00 p.m.

"Has someone called him?"

"We tried, but his cell phone doesn't answer, just goes immediately to voice mail. Again, the ladies said he drove a Chevrolet Impala, several years old, so it would have been equipped with OnStar. We called OnStar to get the number in the car, but the lady at OnStar said but he does not have the service. She said they could locate where the car was by satellite, but we wanted to wait to see if that's what you wanted to do."

"We could, then notify the Highway Patrol to pull the car over and give the bad news, but what would that serve right now? They might even have a wreck on the way home. How could you drive after hearing your wife had been killed? No, it's better just to wait for them to get home. Maybe they left the meetings early and will make it here before long."

"Right," he said. He gave a big sigh. "Let's get this show on the road."

Before they moved, Eric spoke up quietly.

"She was lucky, you know."

"Lucky?" Colton asked. "Why do you say that?"

"Well, maybe I watch too many home invasion movies, also, but doesn't this type of thing usually end in mutilation, beatings, rape, other savage acts to the body? Maybe torture before the person dies?"

"If you put it that way, then, yes, she was lucky. Her death this way would have been instantaneous, a simple bullet to the heart."

But they both were thinking that no death is lucky.

He turned back into the dining area. The forensics team was still lined up along the far wall.

"I want every square inch, no, every *millimeter* of this area combed and cleaned with a fine-toothed comb. Every dust particle, every piece of hair, dander, dust, anything, I want bagged as evidence. Do it slowly and systematically. Then vacuum and save the bag. Comb and vacuum the dog. Maybe it bit the intruder before it was shot. It's not likely, of course, but you never know. I have a feeling we'll need every lucky break we can find. We all know that most crime scenes like this reveal even minute clues. The killer always leaves something behind and that something, however small, will lead us to him.

"There's one last thing, something very important."

He had suddenly thought of something just a moment before. It sounded crazy, even to him, but anything was possible.

"Pull out several hairs with the follicles, from the dog and bag them as evidence. Don't lose them. Another last thing. Take the prints of the woman who found the body. She was the one who opened the back door, right? And the other woman who used the phone on the counter to call 911."

A couple of the men nodded.

"We need to rule out her prints on the knob. Any others, we find out who they belong to. Now, I'll leave you to it."

The forensic techs looked at each other. They were wondering why they had to collect hairs from the dog, but one would do it, being careful to identify and tag the evidence bag.

Chapter 5

As they walked to the back door, there were obvious signs on the tiled floor that the killer had wiped up all footprints the best he could. The towel or whatever that was used was nowhere to be found.

They walked out the back door, which was open. They did not touch it, of course, but visually examined it as they went. No forced entry. It had indeed been unlocked, just as the ladies had told Leonard, who had arrived first on the scene. He pushed the side nearest the kitchen back and forth a couple of times. It moved very smoothly, with hardly a sound. If the killer had moved it ever so slowly, probably not even the dog had heard it open. Or, at least the dog didn't hear a sound until it did and it was too late.

He could picture it asleep on the bed with the woman, then jumping down at the last minute. The killer had probably already stepped into the house.

Did the killer know there was a dog in the house? Had he been surprised when he heard a bark? Whichever, the death of the dog was accomplished quickly and efficiently. It would have the same bullet in it as the woman. But if the killer had known about the dog, that meant that the person was probably someone who knew about the parsonage, the floor plan, perhaps, and someone who knew the pastor's wife personally.

A question came to mind. How many people around here could hit a moving dog with so much accuracy? That would be hard for an amateur using a gun for the first time.

He thought again that the killer must be a marksman.

The two men walked across the road to the church, where the two women who found the body were waiting. Colton wanted to talk to the one who had found the dead women.

It turned out she was the church organist.

No, she didn't know anyone that would harm Maureen. No, she had never heard anyone speak ill of the woman.

Both women agreed about that.

While the two women found all the church membership records, Sunday School attendance records, and any other lists of people associated with the church they could think of, even a church directory, Colton asked them a few questions.

"So, what's going on inside the church? Does the church have any problems?"

The woman, Kelli, who found Maureen, answered first.

"I imagine every church has its set of problems. I've never heard of a Baptist church that doesn't have first one group, then another group, complaining about the first group, and so on. Someone on some committee or another doesn't agree with the rest of the group, usually over something silly like the color of the padding on the pews, something like that."

She grinned.

"But no one you can think of that caused more trouble than anyone else, on a regular basis, maybe?" he asked. He hoped to approach it from a different angle. He wanted one or maybe both of these women to maybe inadvertently say something that might give a clue to the identity of this killer.

He should have known it would not be that simple.

"Just like I said, the usual complaints. But I don't think there was anything that would cause anyone to want to kill Maureen, if that's what you're getting at."

She looked over at the other woman.

"Nothing like that," Janice agreed. "Disagreeing over what music to have for the worship service, or what literature to order to teach the children, does not a murderer make."

Colton gave up. These two were not going to say or commit to anything. He took the copies from the ladies. He could find out all the information he needed about the church members and attendees from the pastor when he talked with him.

Chapter 6

The three men were laughing, reliving moments of the past week that made them laugh. Of course, there were also moments that were quite serious. The pastor was driving. As they drove north past Dutch Mills on Arkansas Highway 59, they did not even think of looking to the left, up the hill at the church or the parsonage. It was summer and the trees lining the small creek and into the community mostly obscured the view, anyway.

Their main concern now was getting home.

About a half mile north of Dutch Mills, they turned right (you can't turn left) on Arkansas Highway 45. Another two miles took them to the home of the first man to arrive home. He got out of the car. Another half mile the two remaining men arrived at the other passenger's home, where the pastor turned around to head back to Dutch Mills.

The man's wife rushed out of the door, waving her arms.

"Jennings, Jennings, wait, please wait!" she shouted.

But Jennings was already on his way. He wanted to get home to his wife and his own bed.

"What is it, what's wrong?" her husband asked.

"Someone has murdered Maureen," she answered, almost choking. Kelli just called me. "She said something about a robbery gone wrong, or something like that."

Keith dropped his suitcases. He ran toward the house. He shouted to his wife, "I have to go to him. Somebody needs to be with him at a time like this."

Before she could pick up a suitcase to take it in, the garage door was rolling up. The car backed out with barely enough room to spare at the top.

Jennings drove along, ready for the week to be over. It had been a good week, but he was thinking how good it would be to get home, kiss his beautiful wife, and sleep in his own bed tonight. There certainly was something to the saying "there's no place like home."

"Home" for the past two years had been the parsonage belonging to Dutch Mills Church. It was just across a driveway, or lane (because it continued on past the cemetery to a house at the end), which meant the church members thought they could come over any time of day, any day. After all, it was their house, wasn't it? Their money built it.

Most of the time he tried not to think about the fact that it did not belong to him and his wife. A person has a tendency to put down roots if a house belongs to that person.

When he turned right into Dutch Mills (you can't turn left) and was across the bridge over the small creek, past a couple of trees, he saw several cars parked at the top of the hill, by the parsonage, and one by the church. The garage door was up, providing some lighting, as well as the headlights of the vehicles. It was hard to make out what kind of vehicles they were through the heavy rain that was coming down.

Oh, no, what is wrong? he wondered. *"Has the church been broken into? Maybe someone thought we leave money in the church. There certainly is nothing else anyone would want, unless you count the new copy machine. Then, what?*

Any equipment in the church was insured, so he had no concern about that. He did, however, have a nagging feeling in the pit of his stomach as he gunned the car to make it up the hill to the parsonage.

One of the cars was a Washington County Sheriff cruiser. He read that when the headlights hit the first vehicle. The other was the Range Rover belonging to the sheriff himself. This he recognized.

What was the big dog doing here?

"Since when does the sheriff himself investigate robberies?" he said, out loud. "Something else has to be going on. Darn that stupid cell phone, dying, not matching anyone else's power cord. Someone would have called me about whatever has happened here."

As he pulled in beside the cruiser, two men were already waiting. They had been watching and waiting for the pastor to arrive. One of the ladies that found the wife had described the car to them. They had waited for several hours now, but they wanted to be the ones to give him the bad news.

You never knew how anyone would react in a situation like this.

Jennings looked at first one and the other, then back again. He knew by the looks on their faces that this was bad news.

"What?" he asked. "Tell me."

He looked around.

"Where is Maureen?"

It had finally dawned on him that she was not there to greet him after he was gone for a week.

"Pastor," Sheriff Colton began. "We have some bad news…"

The feeling in the pit of his stomach hit him like a brick. He gasped.

The man was continuing…

"I'm sorry, but there was an…intruder…in your house last night. We figure he was surprised, maybe in the process of a robbery. He shot your dog…"

Oh, that's okay, he thought. It was Maureen's dog, anyway. He never liked it.

"…and, well, I'm sorry, but…there's no easy way to tell you this, but your wife was shot, also. She's dead, Pastor, I'm sorry."

"What? *What?*" he asked. He wasn't sure he was hearing this.

His knees buckled. The two men caught him as he fell.

"Are you sure? Let me see. She can't be dead. She just can't be!"

He was distraught, as the two men knew he would be. They still held him. He was limp in their grips.

He rose up.

"Let me see her, I have to see her. I don't believe you. This is some kind of nightmare I'm having, and I'll wake up any moment now. It can't be happening."

He tried to twist away from them, but they held on.

"Where is she? In the house? I need to see her."

"No, sir, she is at the Washington Regional Medical Center. In the morgue. The coroner ordered the…her…to be put there because we could not reach you earlier. We do not leave a body on the crime scene like that."

"Crime scene? Crime scene? What do you mean? Oh, yeah, the burglar. But she would have let him take whatever he wanted. She would not have fought him. She knows better than that. Let me go. I have to get to Fayetteville, to the hospital. She's so far away from me. Let me go!"

About that time his friend, one of the men he had let out at his home, pulled into the driveway. He ran to them. He took one of Jennings' arms from the deputy.

"I'm here, Jennings, Martha called to you, but you were already on your way. She told me the bad news. I came right away. You drove fast, or I would have caught up with you. I'll be here with you."

Jennings didn't protest.

"Let's go inside, out of this terrible rain," the sheriff said, trying to steer them toward the house.

They were not listening to him.

"No, I can't go in there. I want to go to the coroner's office right away."

"Let's go, I'll take you to Fayetteville," Colton said. "You both can go with me."

Jennings cried all the way to the hospital, yelling and screaming, wondering why this had happened to Maureen, to them. What was the reason? The purpose? Where was God in all this?

They had just recently finished seminary, him with a ministry degree and her with a music degree. This had been their first place as pastor. They had accepted this small church because it had been available. It was halfway between the West Coast, where they had attended seminary, and their home town in Florida.

"Go, Gators," he almost said aloud. He almost laughed at the thought. It always came so automatically to both of them when referring to their alma mater. Keith would not have understood why he laughed, though, in the face of all that was happening, so he was glad he didn't.

Halfway there he settled into a stony silence, his head leaning against the passenger side window.

Colton thought he might have gone into shock. He knew he probably would have, learning abruptly, after a good, fun week, that his wife had been killed by a burglar. No one knows how they would react to something like that unless it happens to them.

He shook his head. He glanced over at the pastor every so often to make sure he was okay.

The week *had* been a good one. The three of them had been voted by the church to represent the church at the state convention of their denomination. This year, it took place in Little Rock. It moved from place to place, year after year. The convention center in any particular city just had to house around 15,000 delegates. The meetings lasted all week. Any petition before the church that any member of any church had brought forward was presented. Sometimes these were serious concerns, sometimes they were just frivolous, but everyone had to be voted on. That was the tedious part of the meetings, but they had to be lived through to enjoy the good parts of the week.

When they pulled in the lot outside the morgue, they were met by the coroner. The sheriff had called to say they were on the way.

Jennings could barely contain himself while he identified the body. He knew he had to make funeral arrangements, though, and he let the attendant know the name of the funeral home some of the church members used. After he called their family, they would decide if they would take her back to Florida, or not. He thought they would probably want to do that. He couldn't see a reason, at this point in time, to stay in Dutch Mills, much less put Maureen to rest in the cemetery there.

He realized that was a first, gut-wrenching reaction, though, so he would need time to think about it and decide. Whether to stay for a while at the church, he meant. He knew they would probably take Maureen back to their hometown, so her family would always be near and could visit her gravesite. It would be important to them to be able to do so.

Maybe he could find a church around there, also. Right now, though, he had no heart for doing what he had always thought was God's work. He felt his heart closing in on him.

He had no desire to preach right now and had no idea when he would again, ever.

Chapter 7

She puttered silently around the kitchen. She was waiting for her sister to wake up. She stayed as quiet as possible, so she did not wake her.

Presently, her sister did appear in the kitchen door.

"Hi, Sis, did you finally decide to get up?" she asked her, teasingly.

Diane yawned.

"I can't believe I slept so long. Why didn't you wake me up? What was in that hot chocolate we had last night?"

Karen just laughed. "You know what they say. If a little warm milk before bed helps a person sleep, surely hot chocolate does, also. Why don't you get dressed while I get the coffee going?"

When Diane returned to the kitchen, she spotted the Danishes and other pastries in the middle of the table.

"Oh, those are my favorites! You remembered," she said.

"Of course, I did. I even went out in the rain early this morning to buy them for you from a favorite local bakery here. Oh, before I forget. I had to take your car. I hope you don't mind, but mine had a flat tire. I had to get in and out in the pouring rain, so I have a fan going right now, to make sure the side of your driver's seat is dry. And don't worry, I unscrewed the overhead light, so your battery won't wear down."

"Oh, that's fine," Diane replied. "I'd let you borrow it anytime to get these goodies!"

"That's not all you can have, of course," Karen said. "There's bacon, eggs, I can cook whatever you want. This is your short vacation, remember? You deserve to be pampered."

Diane laughed.

"You're too good to me. And, yes, I needed a change of scenery and some relaxing time. I'll take some bacon."

Diane poured them some coffee while Karen cooked the bacon. They took their time over breakfast, or brunch, as they called it. They mostly talked about their mother, who had passed away several years before.

Karen's husband had passed away about six months previously, so they talked about how she was coping by herself. She seemed to be fine living alone now.

"Why don't you decide which games we want to play while I clean the dishes and straighten up?" Karen said. "But you probably know what I want to play."

They had promised themselves some game time. They had grown up playing many types of board games at their mother's house and continued to do so through the years when they visited her.

"I know, I know. *Careers*, right?"

"Now, how did you guess?" Karen asked, laughing.

Careers it was. Karen liked playing this so well that Diane had bought her the game for last Christmas. This was the new board, though, so Diane had brought the old board when she came.

The cat curled around Diane's legs when they sat down at the table.

"Hi, Mommie," she said to the cat. She reached down to pet the cat. She looked up at Karen.

"I'm so glad you took Mommie-cat home with you after mom died. I couldn't bear the thought of her being just left out in the woods by herself. You know how mom was always concerned about her."

"Neither could I," Karen agreed. "Fortunately, she was so used to me, that when I called for her that last day we were at the house, she came running out of the woods to me. The only unfortunate thing was that she had to leave the nice, fat, juicy mouse she had in her mouth. She was bringing her contribution to the family food stores, of course."

They both laughed. Their mom's cat had been an "outside" cat. Their mother did not believe in having animals in the house. She was fortunate that Mommie-cat had such a beautiful coloring of black, grey, off black, that she blended into the woods. If she were still and quiet, you could not even tell where she was.

"The only thing I worried about for those three years mom had her was the fact that she crossed that open field behind mom's house or came down State Line Road in the middle of the day. There were hawks out there, you know, and Mommie is a small cat, even with all that long, fluffy hair."

"Yeah, she was a lucky cat," Diane agreed.

"And I don't think she misses being outside even for one minute. She's made a wonderful house cat. I just think maybe she misses her mice!"

They laughed.

They had just opened the board, distributed the money and set up the board when the phone rang.

Karen answered.

She listened for a minute or two. Her eyes grew wider as her friend continued. Then Karen said, "You've got to be kidding me! That's terrible! I can't believe something like that has happened! Nothing like that ever happens there."

Karen listened a few more moments.

"Is that what they think? That it was a robbery gone bad, that the robber panicked, or something like that?"

She listened.

"Please, Kelli, just calm down. I know nothing like that ever happens there, but, no, I don't think anyone is going to think you did it. Why should they?"

More listening. Karen nodded every once in a while, agreeing with her friend, as if Kelli could see it.

Diane had looked up at her and wondered what the matter was.

"I know you didn't like her and you two didn't get along, and yes, everyone else knew it, too, but there are lots of people everywhere, who don't like someone they know, or even someone they don't know, but that doesn't mean they kill them. That's pretty drastic. Look, just go lie down for a while, relax your body and calm down. You know if you keep being upset over something that wasn't your fault will get you totally stressed out. Go, okay?"

A few more nods.

Karen's friend talked for several more minutes, with Karen interjecting an incredible "what?" "how?" every once in a while.

Finally, the friend hung up.

"What is it?" her sister asked. "You look like you've seen a ghost."

Karen still looked shocked.

"It's the most incredible thing. And in little Dutch Mills, the last place you would think something like that would happen."

"What, what?" Diane asked. "Tell me. Don't keep me in suspense here."

"Oh, sorry," Karen said. "You won't believe this, but the pastor's wife at the church there in Dutch Mills has been killed. They think it was probably a robbery, she woke up, and the intruder shot her. He shot the little dog,

also, my friend guessed so it would not bark and wake up
the woman.

"And there are no clues. You know how it rained here
last night, and still raining now, of course. Well, it seems
it happened during the storm, so all footprints, tire prints,
things like that have been washed away. There was evidence of wet on the dining room floor, which has a sliding
glass door at the back, but the intruder had the presence of
mind to wipe the floor, so there is nothing to use as evidence."

She just sat there, apparently still stunned at this news.

Diane was almost speechless at the news. She finally
found her voice.

"In little Dutch Mills? That is scary. We live only three
miles away."

"I know, I know. You'd better call Wayne and tell him
to lock his doors. The killer is obviously still out there.
Maybe a neighbor, who knows?" Karen asked.

"Well, let's play anyway, okay? There's nothing we
can do."

Diane called her husband. He had not heard the news,
but he did lock his doors.

They played two games of *Careers*. Diane won each
game, but not by much. She would never know that Karen
had several opportunities to use her cards to make better
moves and win the game each time, but rolled the dice
each time, taking the chance to land on a "bad" space,
which she did.

Diane was happiest when she won. She had complained
through the years how Karen always won. Karen decided
this trip to let Diane win, but try not to look so obvious
about it.

They played three games of *Yahtze*, best two out of
three, which Diane won, also. Karen made less than good
judgments here, also, so Diane had a better chance at

winning. You couldn't control the roll of the dice, but you could decide where to place your numbers on the score card. Karen just simply did not make the upper bonus two times.

Aw, what sisters would do for sisters!

As they played, they continued to talk about the murder in Dutch Mills. They wouldn't talk about it for a while, then all at once, one of them would wonder something about it.

They speculated on every possible scenario. The bottom line was, who would do such a thing to a pastor's wife? Or, did he even know it was a pastor's wife?

They ended on a positive note, saying they would get together more often, with more "sister-bonding" time like this.

Diane did not go home until the next morning, which was Saturday. It had still been raining so much the evening before that she decided to stay one more night. She did not like driving in the dark, so driving in the rain in the dark was certainly out. Also, she wanted to be at home Sunday morning to be able to go to church with Wayne.

This rainstorm had been going on for several days. It seemed like it was just stalled over the whole area. It had turned into a real soaker.

Chapter 8

Sheriff Colton was in his office bright and early on Sunday morning. He had agreed with the pastor that he would pick him up at the Northwest Regional Airport when the man returned at the end of next week.

The coroner agreed to get right to the autopsy so the wife's body could be flown back to Florida, their home state, for burial. Cause of death had simply been made as gun shots to the heart. She had died instantly.

It would be a hard airplane ride back to the family, it just had to be done, that's all. The pastor would fly on the same plane with the casket.

Colton agreed with that, as long as the pastor promised to return, which he promised to do.

This was not Colton's usual routine, but this had not been his usual Friday and Saturday. Sundays were always family time—going to church at times, Sunday dinner at his mom's with his brother and his family. The children playing with their cousins.

Mom always provided a full meal. Today was going to be his favorite, fried chicken, mashed potatoes and giblet gravy, corn, and her famous homemade rolls. She had even made his favorite—coconut cream pie.

The routine for Washington County was usually only its share of drunks, drug arrests, domestic violence cases, restraining orders, small-time robberies that were only misdemeanors. At least the kegger frat parties on the University of Arkansas campus fell under the jurisdiction of the Fayetteville Police.

The largest bust they ever made out in the county was a homemade meth lab in an old dilapidated trailer sitting out in the middle of the forest back in the boonies. There had been three of those in the past five years. Two they busted, but somehow the cooks at one of them got wind of them coming, pardon the pun, so by the time they arrived at the clearing in the woods, the trailer was gone. Oh, sure there were signs of recent traffic, the trampled down grasses and unidentifiable tire tracks, but nothing else.

Maybe they moved on to the next county, probably a few miles into Oklahoma. The terrain in the southwest part of this county was thickly forested.

Rarely, but rarely, was there a murder like this. In fact, during the previous five years, this was only the third murder of this type, and those were spur-of-the-moment killings of passion.

A lover's quarrel, or a triangle lover's quarrel, whatever.

There had never been what seemed to be a premeditated murder like this. Colton felt for sure it had been carefully thought out. Now he just had to prove it and that was going to be the hard part.

While they waited for the pastor and husband to return home Friday night (was that just two days ago?), he looked at the membership he had one of the ladies to copy off for them. There turned out to be "active" and "inactive" rolls. She explained that "active" were those who more or less regularly attended the services and participated in the activities of the church, but the "inactive" were those that had dropped out of attendance. Oh, she added, they still lived around there, usually, but they had just "backslid" and no longer came.

He thought that was an interesting choice of words. He was not Baptist, but he always thought the terms and phrases used from church to church were quite unique. Why the people who chose another path could not just be described as no longer attending there, instead of judged as being "backslidden," eluded him.

To each his own, he thought, in reference to religious preferences. He never judged anyone on that score.

The woman had also given him a church directory, which contained photos of those members and some non-members, but still those who attended the church at the time, which in this case was three years ago. Names and addresses were beside each photo.

Good old Olan Mills and those church directories. Maybe this would help make his work easier with this case. She'd gone through and made big "Xs" beside three of the photos. One was of a single mom with a small child, who had taken a job in Springdale, so they moved up there about a year ago and no longer attended. Another was of a young couple with two small children. The husband/father had transferred to Pocahontas with his company, about a year and a half ago, so they were "out."

At least that's what she said.

The third photo was of an older couple. They had moved away about two years before when the woman's mom passed away. The mom had lived in Dutch Mills, down the highway about three miles. They had built a small home on the same property, but had no reason to stay when the mom passed.

They didn't have any reason to come this far to church. She knew they had started attending a church there. Besides, the husband died about six months ago, so this couple was "out," also.

Again, according to the woman.

Boy, she sure is talkative, Colton thought. *Ask one question and get the answers to a dozen. But maybe that's good in this case, who knows?*

Those church roles and the directory were in front of him on the desk right now.

He would still have to talk to these people.

He read about the church.

Chapter 9

The church and community both had an interesting history, really. The community had originally been called Hermansburg in 1883 for the German settlers who first came there. It was one the Butterfield Train Stagecoach routes. The small church had been built on the hill overlooking the community, as they often were in those days. It was white board, on a poured concrete foundation. The original part was the sanctuary and below that was the basement, only accessible from the outside, where the original classrooms for Sunday School were held.

The land was donated and there were several "founding fathers" and their families.

Funds for the building materials were provided by the families who'd originally attended. Men from the community, whether they attended the church or planned to attend, helped build the church. The women provided meals and drinks for the men as they worked.

There were originally two churches that came together to form this one church. One was located about six miles south on the now highway, then just a horse-and-buggy dirt trail. Several families from both churches came together, because of mutual beliefs, to form this church.

They were always mission-minded, so they joined the Baptist Convention before the turn of the century. This was the convention the pastor and two representatives from the church had attended.

For several years services were conducted on both Saturday and Sunday, two times a month. The pastor came into Lincoln, a town nine miles to the north, on the train early Saturday morning. Both days were worship days.

The church building was used for a public school house for many decades. During the 1930s, more and more people attended because more people moved to the area. Several Bible study groups had formed and a vacation Bible school started.

Additions were made to the church over the years and now a new, modern addition had been added to the side of the church, leaving the original sanctuary where it was.

The community through the years supported several grain mills, thus the re-naming of the community. It had general stores, a post office and gas stations. There was always a resident doctor in the area.

Along with the flour and grain mills there were sawmills and blacksmith shops. During the 1930s a canning factory was added, which provided employment for many of the locals for many years after that.

He thought the minute he saw it as he travelled through the county that first month that it was a cute little church. He thought the members must be proud of it. It had the old look about it as well as the modern addition. He wondered at the time how that came about. Usually a whole new building was constructed but used the same name.

He wondered if now it harbored a killer in the guise of a faithful church member.

During the night he decided to map out the addresses in an orderly fashion to avoid too much back-tracking. He had a map of the county on the desk. This mapping was to implement his "dog hair" investigation. The men and one woman on his staff didn't know it yet, but they would be interviewing homeowners and vacuuming vehicles. He was sure it wouldn't be the most popular investigation, but it had to be done.

At least it was a place to start the investigation. People would start clamoring soon enough about clues and what evidence did they have, had they found the killer, and on and on. He could say the investigation was "ongoing."

In reality, the severe weather had totally wiped out any clues or evidence they might ordinarily have found in a case like this. At the very least they would, maybe, find a stray, or partial, print of the bottom of a sport shoe, or something.

But, no, nothing so easy this time.

Yesterday had been spent at the forensic lab. He had a specialty degree in forensic science, so he helped put even the minutest particle they had collected in separate bags to process and analyze. He took the vacuum cleaner bag and had processed even the smallest piece of dust from the home, to show them how he wanted it done. There were going to be so many little brown paper bags on several tables, that he knew it would take them weeks and weeks to go through everything. But, then, it was their job, and what else would they be doing? Having fun with their families and loved ones, perhaps? In a way he felt sorry for the lab techs.

He had laid out for them the way he wanted the contents of the bags to be processed, then left them with it. They were to make regular reports. The first bags would probably come in by the following Wednesday.

As he worked yesterday, he had silently chanted, please, please, something, please. Let us find something, please!

What he needed was a piece of that fried chicken. The thigh was his favorite piece.

He gave a big sigh and opened the map of the county. He started with the directory.

The next time he looked at the clock, it was almost 1:00 in the afternoon.

Wow! he thought. *How time flies when you're having fun!*

Just then the phone rang. It was his wife, offering to bring over a plate, plus a big piece of the coconut cream pie. That was the best idea he had heard today! He realized how hungry he was. He had skipped breakfast to get to the office and get started on this idea of his of interviewing everyone on the lists.

Maybe he bit off more than he could chew. He would soon find out.

The food was just what he needed, then back to work.

Chapter 10

Colton needed to talk about this case, so he decided to call his former chief deputy in Yellville, Arkansas. The deputy had become interim sheriff when Colton left, but ran for sheriff in the general election and won by a landslide.

Colton explained to Clark about gathering the tiniest jot and tittle of evidence from the crime scene, down to the millimeter. He went on to explain his idea about the dog's hairs, that perhaps even one hair from the dog body would have attached to the killer's clothes or body or *somewhere*, somehow, and that just might be the evidence, found in someone's car that could lead to the killer.

"Wow!" Clark said, "now that *is* a theory, I have to admit, but I would say it is a long shot, at best. If I recall correctly, I was watching The Weather Channel that night about the hurricane from the Gulf and how it was expected to hit that side of Arkansas then go northwest, then hook back over Northwest Arkansas again. That western side of Arkansas, right over Washington County, was having a helluva severe thunderstorm. Don't you suppose any hairs would have washed off the person by the rain after he left the house?"

"I've thought of that, but I also thought maybe the killer had an umbrella that he left on the patio by the back door. That patio has a small covering over it, although that night the rain was so heavy and the winds so straight-line, that the whole concrete floor was flooded. But maybe, just maybe, I think, a hair stayed attached, maybe down inside a glove, in a pocket if he put his hand in one, in a cuff, under a collar and was protected that way from the weather, then fell off in a vehicle, whatever.

"I hope that maybe, when the dog was shot, the impact made some hairs scatter. I know, I know, it sounds crazy. But, hey, I've got to have hope in something, you know, and sometimes it's the strangest things, the odd coincidence, that catches the killer. Haven't you watched enough detective movies and shows to know that?"

He said that jokingly and they both laughed. This gave Clark hope for his friend, that Colton was still able to joke about the situation. There may come a point during this case that Colton would no longer be joking, about anything.

"So," Clark asked, "how are you going about that? Are you actually going to check vehicles somehow?"

"Yep," Colton responded. "I have a list of all church members and attendees at that little church there. Right now, I am sitting here mapping out a route that keeps me from doubling back every second trip, or whatever. I'm going to take a blanket search warrant for authority to vacuum each car. If I take the person, the household, by surprise, at least on the first day, I might find more. Of course, I realize by the first or second vehicle I vacuum, the wife will be standing at the window with her iPhone in her hand, calling everyone she knows to look out for us, here we come.

"Some might even go out and vacuum out their cars, even though they had nothing to do with the murder. You know how a police presence affects some people. They act guilty whether they are or not."

"Yeah, we're big and bad, aren't we?" Clark answered.

Colton could picture the grin on his friend's face.

"We just have to hope our super-duper vacuums are more powerful than the average hand-held car vac or dust buster. I have enough money in the budget that I will go first thing in the morning to Lowe's to buy their most powerful hand-held car vacs. I may be spinning my wheels on this, but at least it will show the people in the county that we are doing something. We don't have to explain why we want to vacuum the vehicles. In fact, it might be better to just let them wonder. Maybe someone will slip up.

"Do *you* have any suggestions on this case? Or, if you think of something later, please call."

Clark was shaking his head. He remembered the nightmare they faced with the Ellison murder. There had also been a thunderstorm overnight then, washing away all tire tracks and footprints. The killer had been smart enough to wipe any fingerprints clean.

"What mile radius around or from the community are you going to check the vehicles? Do you think you will find it close by?"

"I thought I would check a five-mile radius from each direction. Of course, going west is Oklahoma, so I will coordinate with the sheriff in Adair County, to see what help he can give. They might just laugh at me, of course. That area is so thickly wooded, a vehicle could be sitting somewhere and never be seen."

Colton sighed.

Clark heard it over the line.

"You're right, I've probably come up with an impossible theory and even more impossible task with checking vehicles. It's only the third day past the murder, and this must show how desperate I am to find a clue, *any* clue, to help solve this case."

He tossed his pencil onto his desk.

Clark heard that, also. He sensed his friend's frustration and this case had just begun.

"Now, pick up that pencil. You know for a fact that if you don't stay busy with something on this case, it will eat you for lunch and spit you out. And you could be right, we know this business. You never know where and how the break might come. An innocently-spoken word by someone, which reminds you of something, anything.

"A lot of times a person is simply eaten up by quilt at what they have done, either accidently or planned. Maybe the killer will sit on what he's done for a while, even months, or years, then come to you and confess. When he sees that you are leaving no stone unturned to find clues, it will surely scare him."

Colton laughed, again.

"You realize we have always said 'he' when we refer to the killer. Just a common thing to do, I guess," Clark said.

"Yeah, I guess," Colton responded. "Habit, probably. Aren't most crimes like this done by men? I'm very interested in knowing what type the slugs are. They made pretty big holes in her chest. Not the type of gun I would associate with a woman. And the shots indicated the killer might be a marksman, they were so precise and exact. The killer had to have had a perfect aim."

"Good point," Clark admitted. "Just don't overlook those tough farm gals out your way."

"You're right, of course," Colton said. "If they can birth cows and throw around those rectangular bales of hay, they have to be strong. I still relate them to rifles for deer hunting more than anything else."

They talked a few more minutes then hung up. They made plans to get together when they both attended the annual conference for county sheriffs that was going to be held soon in Fayetteville. They finalized some plans, including Clark and his wife staying at Colton's home during the conference. It would give them an opportunity to really hash out this case.

Colton turned back to his desk. By tomorrow he would start seeing some results from forensics pertaining to the crime scene. For now, he would continue this plan, whether it made any sense or not.

Soon enough the wolves would be howling about finding the killer. People out in the country were locking doors they never had before.

It wasn't a time for sitting around. Now was the time for his whole department to look extra busy.

⁓⁓⁓

His plan of attack for the interviews of the church attendees/members finished, Sheriff Colton pushed his chair back from his desk. He stretched both arms above his head as far as he could, first one and then the other.

He stopped by his mother's house on the way home, just to say hello. She told him she had sent the rest of the pie home with the family. He didn't have to worry about it, then, because his three boys would already have it gone.

"Bad case, huh?" his mom asked.

"The worst, I'm afraid," he responded. "I've tried to formulate some plans to try to find some clue to find the killer, but they may be exercises in futility, as the saying goes. But, I have to start somewhere.

"The husband, the pastor, won't be back until Friday. They took the body back to Florida for a service and the burial. That's where they are from. In the meantime, I think I'll interview the people in the houses immediately around the church. Maybe somebody heard or saw something, although it was raining cats and dogs."

He stood up. He needed to get home to his family. He had the best wife, one daughter, and three sons, in the world for understanding the nature of his job, but he didn't abuse his family duties. Although he loved this job, he would rather be at home than on the job, anyway.

"Luck, honey," his mom said, as she hugged him. "Don't work too hard."

He grinned as he walked to his car. As far back as he could remember, his mom had been saying that to first his dad, then to both his brother and him.

But luck would have nothing to do with it.

Chapter 11

Colton wasn't as familiar with this southwest part of the county as other parts. When he had taken this job almost two years ago, he was determined to know all the areas of the county.

They'd moved here because their daughter, their oldest child, decided to go to the University of Arkansas and was accepted. This was now her sophomore year. After she had applied, the three of them, his wife, daughter and he, had traveled over to the university campus from Yellville, where he had been county sheriff for many years. She had been thoroughly impressed by the campus, its activities, and of course, the athletic program.

She wanted to be a cheerleader for the "Hogs."

She was a pretty young lady and came to the campus at the same time as open try-outs for the following year. There were three positions available, those not already occupied by the returning squad. Usually, once a cheerleader, it was yours all four years, even though they went through a routine tryout each year.

One girl had dropped out of school during the spring semester, one had married and moved away, and one was just not able to continue. She had let personal problems get in the way of her studies and activities. She paid the price.

To Colton's surprise, Abby made it, although why he was surprised, he didn't know. But being a high school cheerleader and athlete in small Yellville would be nothing compared to this. He worried about the commitment, how it would affect her time for studying. After all, the tuition here was not cheap. He didn't want to feel he had wasted his money. She just laughed and told him not to worry.

He knew, as soon as Abby started to talk about the University of Arkansas, in her junior year in high school, that he might as well start looking for a position in Northwest Arkansas, whether it would be in law enforcement, or otherwise. He had just been pleasantly surprised when this position came available.

He was sorry for the circumstances that made the position available. Around the same time, the sheriff here in Washington County had been "caught with his pants down."

Literally.

When the last sheriff came here, ten years previously, he had made it one of the department's specialized programs to be aggressive toward prostitutes and the johns they were caught with. For a short time, photos of the johns were even printed in the Fayetteville newspaper, the *Northwest Arkansas Democrat-Gazette*. This caused such a furor, though, when the photos of some of the most prominent citizens of Northwest Arkansas appeared, that this particular part of the program was discontinued.

Wives were furious, threatening to sue the newspaper, which legally had the right to print the photos, under the sanction of the Sheriff's Department. There were more than one divorce and some businesses failed.

Pressure was put on the sheriff to discontinue revealing the johns. Considering some of the country's, not to mention the world's, major corporations had their headquarters in this area, he backed down.

He got the message. He liked his job.

He continued to give everyone tickets, of course, but no more revealing the people involved in whatever act he caught them in.

However, there seemed to be one particular "escort" that was arrested from time to time and brought to the office for booking. After a while, the sheriff was the only one who brought her in.

Several months went by before she was brought in the next time, for solicitation. The sheriff had just returned to the office from two weeks' vacation.

He turned around when he heard her voice. He walked toward her and the officer that had her by the arm.

She saw him.

"This is not supposed to happen, you said so! What am I doing here? Just wait, when you want…"

The sheriff had reached them by that time, taken her away from the other officer, and was leading her toward the booking counter. He leaned in toward her. He was talking to her fast and furiously.

It was obvious that she had too much to drink.

But the damage had been done. Several people heard her comments.

All but one was willing to forget what they heard. This was a man that had served on the force for many years. In recent times, he and the sheriff had butted heads about several programs, mostly over what the agenda of the sheriff's department should be. He had never been keen on this aggressive vice program.

That wasn't to say that he didn't believe in trying to patrol and watch certain lounges and bars out in the county for obvious illicit activities, but he knew this sort of thing had gone on since time began and nothing would completely wipe it out.

So, he convinced a couple of other deputies on different shifts, who did not particularly like the sheriff, either, to start watching the sheriff, following him in their own vehicles. When they knew he had an established routine, at a certain third-rate motel, one night they raided the room.

Since all three of the officers had body cams, there was plenty of evidence against the sheriff. Not only was he caught in the act, but the records showed that each time the lady had been brought in, no charges were filed, and no fines paid.

There were comments of "if you lay down with dogs, you get up with fleas," and that sort of thing.

He had simply fallen victim to human nature. Being around something too long produced too much temptation.

And she was a beautiful woman.

The results were swift and sure, though, for the sheriff. He was asked to resign, effective immediately.

Every morning, for almost a year, Colton checked possible job openings in the Northwest Arkansas area when Abby first expressed an interest in UofA, Fayetteville. He already knew what that meant. For many years now, what Abby wanted, Abby got! She was an only girl, so whenever anything was in the budget, it was hers.

It didn't help, of course, that he had graduated from the University, Fayetteville campus. After his graduation, he applied for several positions in law enforcement around the Northwest Arkansas area, but instead had ended up in Cook County, Illinois. His wife, Marsha, had moved to California right after they both graduated high school, having been "high school sweethearts" and he lost track of her for twelve years, when a bizarre incident brought them together at Midland, Arkansas, just south of Fort Smith. He realized he had never stopped loving Marsha, who had Abby but had never married. He was amazed to find the Abby was his and he and Marsha married. Stints with the Denver Police Force and Marion County, Arkansas, brought them to this location.

Fortunately, Marsha had started saving for Abby's higher education when she was born. It was unbelievable how the cost of tuition had increased everywhere, but at least they had it.

The morning this opening appeared, he did not hesitate in applying. It was an appointed position, which was unusual. In general, this position was an elected one in the county. But a few states still had it as an appointed official. It was an important position, Washington County Sheriff. Because of this, he didn't feel he had a chance of it being offered to him. After all, there were about 250 employees within the department, regular deputies and auxiliary and support staff, so surely it would go to one of them.

He was offered the position! Considering his background, education, and experience, he was the final candidate. He had hoped no one would resent his having been hired. Those types of people would make it hard on a person because they did not receive the promotion they thought they deserved. Usually there was *something*, just one little something, that made the "powers-that-be" hesitate in hiring a person, but the person could never see it in him or herself. An attitude that one *deserved* the job would usually keep that person from getting it.

He didn't find out for about six months that he was appointed because one of his old frat buddies influenced the appointment. He had no reason to look to see who was what in the county administration. The County Commissioner position carried a lot of weight and just happened to have this appointment power. When the Commissioner saw Colton's name and saw the resume, he realized who he was.

Piece of cake.

So, here he was. The counties were about the same in land mass, but in Marion County he'd had a staff of 75, all told. Also, Washington County was the home of

Fayetteville, Springdale, and the University of Arkansas, while Yellville had been the biggest town in the other county. This salary was also substantially higher, so the family would have no worries there, even with a higher cost of living.

But the old friend had been sure he could handle it.

And he could tell Abby was glad her family would be less than an hour away if she needed them. She would never let them know that, of course. They just knew.

They were moved a month before he was to appear at the office and begin his duties. He spent his time wisely.

Loaded with the same county map, 911 map, and even a geological map of the county, he had spent every day, just as if he were at work on the job, driving throughout the county to become familiar with the back roads and "pig-trails" of the county, as one of the deputies called them.

Some days were spent getting to know the men and women of his staff, at lunch and various grill parties at their homes. The favorite meal seemed to be centered around a hog, carefully placed above a burn pit in the ground. The meat was delicious, although watching the hog go around and around was not pleasant for him.

But this was "Hog" country, so this was the thing to do.

Chapter 12

One day found him down a not-so-used lane with grass growing in the middle. He was following the 911 map, identifying each name and number on the mailboxes as he came to them. He stopped at the mailbox, because the only "road" that continued further was about wide enough for an ATV. There was probably a house, or mobile home, at the end, but he could not see anything for the woods. He was not willing to put his Range Rover in danger. It was several years old, but he didn't want it damaged so soon.

This must have been what the deputy meant about a "pig-trail." Colton decided he would only venture further if, or when, he had to. Maybe the people who lived at the end would never cause any trouble, or run a meth lab, or anything.

He had a hard time turning around on this narrow road, but finally made it. He wondered if his power steering would ever be the same.

By the time he had to officially be at the office, he felt he had a good feel for the county ways and byways.

Just not here. He probably had not explored this area as much because it seemed so peaceful, and the epitome of quiet country living at the time he came down this way.

Until now.

Now, the folk around here were locking their doors at night, jumping up during the night when their dogs barked. They just knew there was a killer among them.

Chapter 13

Kelli called her friend, Karen, after church on Sunday evening.

"You wouldn't believe the tension in the church today," she began. "I think I was trembling so hard, it's a wonder I was able to play through the service. It didn't seem like anyone was singing, but maybe I was just concentrating so hard I only heard my own playing.

The preacher was the Director of Missions. That's the only person we could get last minute like this, and he gave up another commitment. But, he felt the church needed to start healing from this terrible ordeal."

Kelli had not paused all the time she was saying this. Karen finally got a chance to get a word in edgeways.

"I suppose they all think the person next to them did it, right? Was everyone looking at everyone else and wondering about it? I still can't believe something like this happened. I will bet, though, that it was just a robbery gone south. I can imagine a burglar panicking when Maureen heard him and started out of bed. You did say she was still in bed when she was shot, right?"

"Right," Kelli said, "and I'll never forget that I was the one to find her. I'll never forget how she looked. And don't think for one minute that I had anything to do with it. You, of all people, know how much I disliked her. But never enough to kill anyone."

Karen sounded shocked.

"Of course, I didn't think, for one second, that you had anything to do with it. Not getting along with someone and murder are two totally different things. You don't have it in you to do something like that. Surely no one at church said anything to you like that, or even hinted at it. That's terrible, if they did!"

She was getting excited. Her voice had raised an octave, at least. She did that when she was agitated.

"No, no, nothing like that happened. Everyone was very subdued, still in shock, I think. Brother Ben tried to put a good face on everything, but I don't know if anyone was listening to what he said. I know I don't remember a word of it."

"Now, don't let this upset you too much, just calm down, okay?" Karen put a soothing tone in her voice. She didn't want her friend upset.

"I just don't want anyone to think I had anything to do with it."

"I'm sure they don't," Karen responded. "You call me and talk about it anytime you want to, okay? Talking about things like this always help. And thanks for calling this time."

Kelli didn't realize she was being told to hang up. She thought it was her idea, and she did.

Karen did not like the fact that her friend was now going to go off the deep end worrying about people thinking she had committed the murder. Kelli was always upset about things, first one thing, and then another.

Karen thought that surely the death of Maureen would allow her to stop worrying.

Chapter 14

They first met when Karen and her husband built a small home just west of Karen's mother's house, across the woods, actually. There was a trail through the woods from one house to the other. They could not see each other's house during the summer because of all the trees and leaves, but during the winter Karen could just barely see the roof of her mother's place.

Her mother's place was behind a slight knoll, almost a ridge, that went north and south. It was part of the same ridge that went through Dutch Mills, where the small church "on the hill," and the parsonage were located. Karen's mother's place was just three miles south of Dutch Mills, located right on the Arkansas/Oklahoma line.

A dirt road went beside Karen's house all the way, three miles, from Arkansas Highway 244 into the little Dutch Mills community, but it was slow going that way. It was rocky. True, the road grader came out occasionally and ran up and down this road, but that only seemed to make the surface worse.

This dirt road had originally been called State Line Road, but had been re-named Dutch Mills South. This change was due to the 911 numbering throughout the county. Easier to find people, Karen supposed, but why not just keep it State Line Road? Everyone knew it by that name, anyway.

After Karen and her husband attended the church the first time after moving there, Kelli had come to visit. Karen wondered who was in the Toyota minivan as it turned into the driveway.

Kelli not only welcomed them to the church, but also proceeded to give them a history and described the two "groups" that seemed to make up the demographics of the church. What one group wanted to do, the other didn't. A discussion had been started about expanding the church. One group, the ones with the most money, no doubt, wanted to expand, while the other group thought the church should stay with its original structure.

This latter group did not think there were enough people attending to pay for an expansion, anyway. Right now the old auditorium was full, but what if people stopped coming? Then, the payment could not be made on the new church.

Kelli was in this latter group. But she not only thought they could not afford an expansion, her great-grandfather had been one of the founding fathers of the church, so she wanted to keep it like it had been from the beginning. These "founding fathers" were called charter members, and not only included men, but some women, also.

Tradition always dies hard.

Karen realized immediately that Kelli wanted her to be on her "side" with any controversy going on, but she also knew when to keep her mouth shut. She would quietly form her own opinion of any and all situations in the church.

It did not take too many Sundays to realize that the pastor's wife did not like Kelli. Karen never heard her say a kind word about her, but usually some form of criticism. Either Kelli had been a half-note behind the music that morning, or had been too loud, or was off with the organ-piano duet the players had attempted. And "attempted" was always said in a critical way.

Maureen must have thought it was part of a pastor's wife duties to criticize the church members she felt fell short of her somewhat skewed standard. Of anything, not just the music.

Unfortunately, somewhere, somehow along the line, she had been made music director.

Unfortunately for Kelli, that is.

In the same number of Sundays it took for Karen to realize that Maureen did not like Kelli, Karen realized that Kelli had more musical ability in one finger (Karen's thoughts) than Maureen would ever have.

Then, somewhere along another way, Maureen started criticizing Kelli for her teaching of the second-grade Sunday School class, an age group that Kelli truly loved to teach. There had been something to do with dinosaurs. Kelli had taught the children about dinosaurs and the age of the earth, that sort of thing.

One of the children had mentioned it to her mother, who told an elder, who told Maureen, who made it her duty to speak to Kelli about it. Maureen had also riled up the elders. After all, didn't they believe that God created the earth in six days, about 6,000 years ago, so how could dinosaurs have even been in the equation?

According to Maureen, Kelli needed to stop teaching, if she were going to say things like that.

When the nominating committee chose teachers for the next year, Kelli did not have the second grade, rather no grade at all to teach.

She was heartbroken. In her educated mind (as was in Karen's), the science surrounding the teaching of dinosaurs fit well within the context of Biblical teachings.

After all, the first five books of the Bible were pre-historic, which meant they were not written down, only passed down through generations and generations, thousands and thousands of years, probably hundreds of thousands of years. Who could say what was the timeframe of these five books and all that was finally written there?

Somehow, throughout the year that Karen and her husband attended the church, Karen was able to stay friends with both "groups." She just stayed friendly, that's all. Probably no one ever knew what she really thought.

But she did become Kelli's friend. They were both educated, intelligent people, as were both the husbands.

Karen hoped that no one at the church would be spiteful enough against Kelli to tell about all these "confrontations" to the sheriff or another deputy. Such talk would lead to undue suspicion on the part of the sheriff.

She didn't want her friend suspected of harming Maureen.

Chapter 15

Driving west from Fayetteville early Tuesday morning after the murder, Sheriff Colton thought how beautiful and clean the world looked. It had stopped raining around noon the day before and it had left the trees and leaves sparkling in the morning sunlight. The sun was behind them for half the way, then on his left (you can't turn right) when he turned down Arkansas Highway 59 toward Dutch Mills. His chief deputy, Eric, was with him. Under no circumstances would he let one of the men or women go out alone, not with this killer still out there.

This countryside was really beautiful. It did not have the same hills that Yellville had, since that town sat in the beginning of the Ozark Mountains. Here, the Ozarks were petering out into what was called the "foothills," the land becoming more and more flat as it went into Oklahoma and the South Central Plains. Still, there were plenty of ridges around and he had to accelerate as he climbed the ridge up to the church at Dutch Mills.

He parked his cruiser under the shade of a large tree at the side of the church. He was not planning to be here long enough to lose the shade. They climbed out of his vehicle and leaned against it, looking east. The sun was not in their eyes because there were plenty of large trees to provide cover.

Colton wanted to get the feel and vibe of this place. There were no other vehicles around. The pastor's car was in the garage, he knew. Jennings, the pastor, had stayed with his wife's body all day Saturday as the coroner made his investigation. He sat out in the hallway in a chair, refusing to leave.

Jennings knew they had to do an autopsy, since she had been murdered, but he couldn't stand the thought of her body being cut up like that. He had no choice. He could choose to stay with her, though.

First of all, the coroner had removed the bullets from her chest. Colton had been present, as well as his chief deputy.

The coroner held up the two bullets for them to see. They were bloody, having come right out of the body.

"Now, that's unusual," Roy, the coroner, said.

"How so?" Colton asked.

"I haven't seen bullets like this in…well…years and years, I know. I'm sure Walmart still sells them, but you would probably have to ask them. They are probably kept under the counter or in the back or something. But I think they might still be available. I don't think they are still manufactured, though, because the gun they fit is not made anymore. It's still a very acceptable gun, just older."

He was still holding up the bullets. Colton and Eric moved closer to inspect the slugs.

"I see what you mean," Colton began. "That's a .22-caliber long, a special cartridge. And you're right again. That fits a long barrel .22-caliber pistol, probably one without a safety. They were dangerous simply for the fact that they did not have a safety on them. Once that trigger is pulled, it's over. It's a very powerful slug, too, not the average .22-caliber bullet."

"Here, look," Roy said, as he held the slug toward Colton. "What else do you see?"

Colton took the bullet.

"Wow! That's homemade, specially made for the gun it was fired from. Maybe that will narrow down the investigation. There can't be too many people around Dutch Mills who make their own bullets and own an older model long-barreled .22-caliber hand gun."

Roy laughed.

"Now, you're not that green, even coming from the Ozarks. Didn't most of the men around there make bullets? Don't ever think they don't around here. It's much cheaper for hunters and farmers to fill their own buckshot and other ammo. If you find a man who *doesn't* know how to do it, or who doesn't have the equipment attached to his work bench out in the barn, *then* you can worry.

"I'll make you a bet," Roy continued. "The gun this bullet fits is now down an old well shaft, totally closed off, or in a crevice that is open, somewhere on the ridge that runs north and south along Dutch Mills toward the Boston Mountains between there and where Van Buren becomes part of that ridge. I've hunted in that area. There are crevices so deep, anything could be dropped into them and never be found. It would probably keep bouncing down to Hell, which is where it belongs, of course. Yep, that baby is in the wind!" he concluded.

"Thanks for the encouragement," Colton said, but not unkindly. "I'll still focus part of my investigation on finding the weapon these belong to. How old do you think the gun would be?"

Roy was around sixty years old. He was born and raised in Northwest Arkansas, just north of Dutch Mills about fifteen miles, in a small community named Cincinnati on Arkansas Highway 59.

Everyone always said "Arkansas" to identify this highway because it started just over the Oklahoma line on the Arkansas side, ranging from about two miles from the

Oklahoma line at Siloam Springs, Arkansas, all the way to Van Buren on Interstate I-40. Actually, it went all the way north up Arkansas to the Missouri line, where it met another highway.

Parallel to this highway, just barely over in Oklahoma, U.S. Highway 59 started on the line in Siloam Springs and went south to Sallisaw, Oklahoma on I-40.

You just had to say which highway you were talking about.

The same ridges and geological ranges covered all this area, so Roy knew what he was talking about.

Colton and Larry both nodded. They understood, also.

But there was always hope that the weapon would turn up somewhere. Since it was an older, unique pistol, maybe the killer would not have wanted to get rid of it, but had kept it for "old times' sake," or something like that. These people were sentimental about their firearms. Weapons were passed down from generation to generation.

"Probably at least forty years old, I'd say."

Colton nodded agreement.

"Before a gun had to be registered, passed down the generations, maybe bought at a pawn shop, and who would remember that or have a receipt now, right?"

"No way," Eric agreed.

"So, what is the official COD?" Colton asked.

"I'll put it on the death certificate as 'gunshot to the chest'," Roy replied.

Chapter 16

For some reason, they both kept leaning against the car. This was Tuesday morning. Yesterday had been spent at the office. Twenty of his deputies had come for a meeting for this particular homicide. They had brainstormed, with several good suggestions from the men and woman as to how to proceed with this investigation.

Assignments were made in certain areas, including Colton passing out maps to the officers. These were maps of sections of the county around Dutch Mills. Four officers, beside Colton and Eric, were assigned only to this case. That's all he thought he could afford to use exclusively on this. They were to go out in twos, for safety, and question each homeowner on the map. If they did not find a particular person home during the day, then they were to make their own schedule to try to interview them during the evening. No home was to be left untouched.

They were given general search warrants to be able to search and vacuum any and every vehicle found at the home, finding out if there were more belonging to the owner, and go to that vehicle/person, also.

There was more than one person who looked at another with raised eyebrows when this assignment was made. Colton explained that they were leaving no stone unturned in this case. Any and every angle, all clues called in, *anything* pertaining to this investigation was to be addressed in detail.

They all knew time was of the essence. The more time between the murder and the discovery of evidence, the less likely there was to be any evidence left to discover.

Colton had assigned himself and his partner the area directly around the church.

It was certainly quiet here. With no traffic going by on Highway 59 just now, the only sounds were those of the birds in the trees.

"Such a beautiful place to harbor such a diabolical plot," Eric said.

"So, you don't believe it was just a burglary gone wrong, caught in the act and panic, all that?"

Colton looked over at Eric.

"For some reason, no, I don't," Eric responded. "It seems more like something that was planned than an act of opportunity. Of course, a burglary could have been planned, I know that, but wouldn't a burglar have come when he knew the pastor and his wife would not be at home? It makes more sense."

"Maybe he thought they had both gone to the church's state convention."

"Just doesn't feel right," Eric said, shaking his head.

Colton agreed, silently. He had always thought that the burglary-gone-wrong angle was not right. But here he was, caught up with the dog's-hair angle. He just couldn't let go of that thought. He knew what some of the squad were thinking. It was a long shot, but he wanted to be able to say, when it was all said and done, that he had explored every angle and every idea possible. He didn't want anyone pointing at him, asking him why he didn't think of this or of that. He wanted to be able to say they investigated this or that.

"I know it's empty and has a For Sale sign in front, but I want us to start with what Mrs. Collins called 'the old parsonage,' the house on the other hill over there, that you see as you turn this way."

He pointed as he spoke. Eric knew the house he was talking about.

"Let's walk," Colton said.

They climbed the steep driveway to the empty house. After peering in the windows and seeing that nothing was in it, they explored thoroughly around the sides and back. No grass was unduly worn, no more than perhaps by the few persons who may have looked at the house, interested in buying it. It was an old house, though. The information he read about the church had said it was built in 1940.

He wanted to look inside, though, so he called the realtor, who said she would meet them at 1:00 with the key.

Next, they walked over to the house that was just at the bottom of the hill below the church, where you either gave your vehicle some extra gas and came up the hill to the church, or made a left-hand turn to go down what was called Dutch Mills South. This was a rocky, gravel road.

Colton knew it went the three miles south to stop at Arkansas Highway 244. This was part of what he had explored that month they moved to Washington County. He had an excellent memory, unless he was super tired, then his brain seemed to shut down. They had not been on this case long enough to be tired. So, he had enough of a memory to know that one time down it was enough. But they had to question everyone in every house down this road.

They also had to question all the people who lived in the three houses down a short road to the north here in the community. This short road stopped at a creek.

Eventually, everyone would get a visit.

Right now, they slowly and cautiously approached this first house. The mailbox read "Carlton" and gave the number. He was ever mindful of dogs that lay in wait, then attacked silently. It had happened to him once and he didn't want to face that again.

There were no vehicles in the driveway, but that didn't mean someone might not be home.

No dogs appeared. However, when they started up the steps to the front porch, two dogs started barking from the backyard. They must have been fenced in, though, because they did not appear, just kept barking.

No one answered their knock. They walked around the house to the side. There were two dogs behind a fence, but they stopped barking when the two men approached that side.

There were three cows in an enclosure. One had a calf with her. There were a dozen or so chickens in another enclosure, so the men knew this house was occupied. The owners were just not here right now. They decided to go back to the car and drive to the next house down the road, which they could see, but was at least a quarter of mile away.

Faster to drive.

They talked on the way back to the car about this part of the county. It might appear at first to be plain country houses and living, but there certainly was more to it than met the eye.

They had taken Highway 62 West out of Fayetteville, through the smaller towns of Farmington, Prairie Grove, and Lincoln. A few miles west of Lincoln, they turned south, or left (you can't turn right), onto Highway 59. This would take them nine miles south to Dutch Mills.

They commented on the huge numbers of chicken houses they saw on the way. These were modern, very long structures, climate controlled by computers.

Watering and feeding the chicks as they grew was also computer controlled. Even the slightest drop in temperature in each house or glitch in the feeding systems, sent a signal to the owner's Smartphone and they were there in minutes. And they had to always be prepared to take care of a problem in a matter of minutes.

This was big business.

Colton had done his homework on this county during the thirty days he came early, before reporting to work.

Poultry, including these chickens, was Arkansas' leading agricultural industry. Many poultry and egg industries were part of this. Arkansas was number three in the nation with Washington County being the leader in Arkansas. There were Simmons and Tyson Foods, to name just two major companies. Most of the signs they had seen were Simmons.

These were broiler houses. They came in as chicks, were grown for six weeks, then collected by the company. The growers were paid by the pound, weighed as they were collected.

Not only was this part of the state a leader in the poultry industry, but Northwest Arkansas was the headquarters of some of the leading corporations in America.

To name just a few, there was Walmart Corporation and Sam's Club, Jones Truck Line, Tyson Foods, J.B. Hunt, and George's Food, Inc. It also was the location of The University of Arkansas, not the little campus it was when Bill and Hillary Clinton attended.

The poultry industry was so important to Northwest Arkansas and Arkansas in general, there was a large building on the University of Arkansas campus devoted exclusively to the science of poultry, The Poultry Department.

Which brought Colton's thoughts to all the personal wealth in Arkansas. First and foremost, of course, were the children of the late Sam Walton, founder of Walmart, with the Hunts high on the Forbes list. There was always Winthrop Rockefeller, an Arkansas governor and billionaire. And, of course, Bill and Hillary Clinton along with many others.

If Arkansas were mentioned in conversation anywhere these days and anyone thought "hillbillies," it meant they were simply out of the loop. There was nothing redneck about the wealth and reputation of Arkansas for quite a few years now.

Colton considered himself lucky to be the sheriff of Washington County and have met some of these people since he was here.

Another advantage to moving here was the fact he had reconnected with all his classmates and frat brothers from the University of Arkansas. This not only was a joy for Colton, but for Marsha, his wife, as well. In the past almost two years they had attended a reunion, numerous grill parties, and there was always the tailgating at the University of Arkansas football games.

Colton wasn't sure how it happened, and he didn't question it, but somehow one of his old buds was able to come up with box season passes for all home games for the entire family. Colton knew enough to know those didn't come cheap, if they came at all. Usually, the people in possession of certain seats were able to keep them from year to year. As he told Marsha, he wasn't about to look a gift horse in the mouth!

Maybe someone of the "powers that be" thought it worthwhile to have the county sheriff at the games, to help with crowd control, if need be, if for no other reason.

Whatever, they enjoyed all the perks the position brought them.

But knowing all this about this area, and all the people he knew, was not going to help them solve this murder.

Chapter 17

They pulled into the driveway of the next house down the road. Since they did not find anyone home at the first house, they should have time to interview the people here, vacuum the one vehicle they could see and be back at the old parsonage by 1:00 to meet with the realtor.

A man came out of the door. He called to two dogs that were barking to "shut up, you old hounds." The dogs immediately slunk around the corner of the house to the back of the house.

Colton and Eric got out of the cruiser.

They introduced themselves and verified the man's name as the same one on the mailbox.

Mr. Frank knew what they were here for, or at least he could guess. He had told his wife that it wouldn't be too many days before the sheriff would be talking to everyone down State Line Road here. Oops, he said, Dutch Mills South. He could never remember that it had been renamed a couple of years back. 911 or something like that. What did that help with all the cell phones, especially having the cell phone tower just up the hill from him, across the road?

He was still mad at old Mr. Jones for allowing AT&T to build that tower. He'd heard that they, the towers, that is, caused cancer, not the neighbor.

Yep, here was the sheriff and a deputy. Been expecting them.

They were home that night, down in the storm cellar. A weird thing, having a hurricane double back and hit in Arkansas, with all those high winds, hail, rain, and a possible tornado or two. Thought they were land-locked. He didn't want to live anywhere near any ocean for any hurricanes to hit his place. Found some of his stuff first in one person's field and then another.

No, no one else with them.

"However, before we could go down into the cellar, I had to go to Stilwell and buy some ice cream for my daughter. She's in the family way, you know, and craves ice cream most of the time. She's seven months along. So, in spite of the high winds, I went into Stilwell to the Walmart before it closed. I knew Walmart would still be open, in spite of the winds and weather report.

"To answer your question as to whether I saw something strange or different that night, I did. When I went out to get the ice cream, there was not an extra vehicle down to Henry's place, just their pickup. But when I went to feed his animals and milk the cow that morning, his son's pickup was there. Guess the bum came home late to sleep off his latest drunk. Henry's had a time with that boy. Hell, ain't a boy anymore. The man's at least twenty-five now, if he's a day. Staggered out of the house and got into his pickup and left while I was in the barn milking the cow. Not sure how he got out of his truck and into the house in all this wind and debris blowing around and all. Guess he just got it lucky to get away while I was milking. Can't stop right in the middle of milking a cow, you know, she wouldn't know what was happening and it might be bad for her udder. I just had to keep on milking.

"I say he was lucky 'cause if I had caught him, I would've given him a piece of my mind for just coming and going like he did. Henry was gone by the time I went to milk and feed. I just hope he woke the son up and sent him on his way. Probably not, though, you know how parents are. Give and give to the kids, and they take and take. Maybe one day they'll wake up and make the bum stand on his own two feet."

Mr. Frank took a breath.

Colton felt the man was in danger of continuing.

The man *was* continuing.

"If you want to know how they got along with the pastor's wife, I can tell you. Well, I don't rightly know about Henry, but the son and that woman have had what you might call a…confrontation…or two in the last year. The son always comes, whenever he comes, day or night, with his radio blaring at the top of the volume. Not only is the volume at top sound, but his bass is turned up. All you can hear above everything else, is a loud 'boom, boom, boom' as soon as he turns off the highway. Know he's coming, for sure.

"Can't sleep when he's coming, day or night. She's probably trying to take a nap during the day, and certainly sleeping during the night, but that noise would carry up the hill, for sure. We can hear it down here at our place.

"The last time he came, well before this one, that is, was during a Saturday night. Well, that did it, of course, since they have to work on Sunday. Only day of the week they work, you know, so they must need their beauty sleep over Saturday night.

"I know all about this because she confronted Henry about it and he complained to me. Seems she actually came right down to the house, right in the middle of the night, and chewed out the son for making all that noise and waking up the whole community.

"He laughed at her, which made her angrier than ever. She told him just what she thought about him and then he got mad, and you can imagine how far south the whole thing went from there.

"Nope, there's, sorry, there was no love lost between Henry and his son and that woman. Sounded like she wasn't understanding at all. Kid's got a problem, but, according to Henry, she didn't care at all. Just ranted and raved about the noise. Went back up the hill in a grand huff, he said."

This is the first good lead I've had, Colton thought. *Maybe we've got lucky right away. Maybe it isn't coincidence that the old man and wife left at the same time as the murder, or thereabouts, or that the son was here at the same time and left at the crack of dawn. Maybe they were even in on it together.*

"I certainly can't say a word like that to this man, though. It would be around the community within minutes that the county sheriff suspected Henry Carlton and his son of murdering the preacher's wife, especially since the wife has had a couple of run-ins with the son about noise or whatever.

"Mr. Frank, I sure appreciate your telling me all this. I'll keep everything in mind. You don't know when the Carltons will be back, do you?" Colton asked.

He needed to get the man back on the subject at hand, although all the info had been very useful.

"Couldn't tell you. They're usually gone for about two weeks, maybe a day or two longer. Probably depends on how well the fish are biting."

"Oh, so you know where they are?" Colton asked. He hoped to be able to talk to the Carltons right away.

"No, Henry's just mentioned about fishing, wherever they go. Seems the fishing can be good or bad, even at the same time of the year. They go about three times a year, too, you might want to know that. Always ask me to help with the animals when they go."

Colton was disappointed. It looked like they would have to wait until the couple returned.

"Do you mind if we vacuum your pick up? We have a warrant."

The deputy produced the warrant.

"My pickup? Why the pickup? Is the pickup the killer?" The man chuckled like he was being funny.

"No, of course not," Colton answered. "We are just investigating every angle."

They knew that everyone down this road would know in the next few minutes that the sheriff and his deputy were vacuuming vehicles. They just wouldn't know why, of course, so if someone thought they had something to hide, and tried to clean out their vehicle, it wouldn't be an unseen dog hair!

"If you don't know when Mr. and Mrs. Carlton are returning and have no way to contact them, what do you do in case of emergency?" Colton asked. Did anyone leave their home like this, with no way of contacting them? Who did that?

"Guess he expects me to call the county fire department if there's a fire or call the vet if one of the animals gets sick. There's a volunteer fire department about six miles south in Evansville and the vet we all use over in Stilwell makes house calls and would charge Carlton for the bill. I would, too. Make all the necessary calls, I mean, not send him a bill. Then we would just wait 'til they return and get the bad news. Nothing's never happened, though."

"Okay," Colton responded. He handed the neighbor one of his business cards. "Please give me a call the very minute they return, okay? I need to talk to them as soon as possible."

"Will do, Sheriff," the man agreed.

They left. It was time to meet the real estate agent at the old parsonage on the other side of the church. Well, it was down the hill, then a narrow valley, then up the hill to the old house.

Colton didn't expect to find any evidence there, but they made a thorough inspection of the inside and outside of the house with the agent.

They had time to go to one other house past the Franks. It was on the opposite side of the road, with a short driveway up a hill, the same type of drive that took a person up to the church. This side of the road was part of that ridge that went several miles to the south. Just over the ridge would be the State of Oklahoma.

The mailbox said Jones, which would probably be the man Herman Frank had complained about, the one with the AT&T tower in his backyard.

Besides from a complaint about Herman Frank by Mr. Jones along the same line that Frank had complained about Jones, the interview was uneventful. Jones and his wife had been at home, asleep that night. They got up about their usual 6:30 a.m. the next morning and went about their usual routine.

He was just as surprised as Mr. Frank about having his car vacuumed but had no complaints.

They had two dogs and Colton was sure that would be the hairs found.

It was time to return to the office and fill out the day's report.

Chapter 18

The first week of the investigation went by without much being discovered. The two other teams assigned to the "hair-brained theory" had kept to their assigned areas as much as possible, turning in the evidence bags from the vacuum cleaners as directed.

It was time to pick up the pastor at the airport.

They traveled west from the Northwest Arkansas Regional Airport toward Gentry, Arkansas, where they would turn south on Arkansas 59 and straight to Dutch Mills on the same highway.

Thanks to the efforts of Alice Walton, daughter of Sam Walton, the founder of Walmart, this exceptional airport had grown into its own. Executives from around the world came into this facility, largely due to Walmart. Built in the little community of Highfill, between Rogers and Gentry, Arkansas, it was a boon to the whole region.

It was only seventeen miles northwest of Fayetteville, convenient to those sports fans and supporters of the "Hogs" of the University of Arkansas. There were non-stop flights to many of the major cities in the United States and the pastor's had been one of them. It had been unthinkable to transfer Maureen's coffin from plane to plane.

With the tremendous growth of the Northwest Arkansas area, the smaller Drake Field, located at the southern edge of Fayetteville, had simply proved inadequate to handle the amount of traffic coming into the area.

The trip from airport to Dutch Mills would give the sheriff and his deputy about an hour and a half with Jennings. This would be the first opportunity they had to question the pastor about the whole situation. He was not in a state at first to even think about answering questions.

The usual greetings out of the way, Colton felt the time had come for some answers.

"Pastor, you know I have to ask you some questions concerning your wife's death, don't you? I hate to do it, but it's necessary."

"Well, of course, sure," Jennings answered. He didn't know what sort of questions the sheriff might want to ask.

"First of all, can you think of anyone who might want to harm your wife?"

Jennings was startled. A fleeting face went through his mind, but it was so fleeting, less than a split-second, even, that he lost the thought as soon as it came.

He frowned.

The frown was not lost on Colton.

"What? Did you think of someone?" he asked.

"I…no…I was startled by the question, that's all. Why would you think anyone would want to harm her? This was just a burglary gone sideways, wasn't it? She was starting to catch him in the act, and the burglar reacted? Wasn't that what it was? Are you saying it could have been something else? Something *more*?"

"We have to investigate all possibilities, especially when a weapon like a gun is involved. That's why we have to ask such difficult questions, which I apologize for, of course."

Colton was trying to give the pastor as much consideration as he could. It couldn't be easy to respond to such a question.

"Anyone?" he repeated.

"Not anyone I can think of with such a bad feeling toward her that she would murder her. That's unthinkable!"

"You said 'she.' Does that mean you thought of someone?"

"There were just little conflicts here and there with different people, some church members, some members of the community. But, like I said, nothing that would lead to murder, I'm sure."

Colton wasn't so sure. Sometimes even the simplest thing to one person could be blown up in the mind of another until it was uncontrollable. Road rage was like that. One driver was usually willing to go on when a confrontation occurred, while the other driver actually started stalking the other with his vehicle. Sometimes such actions led to serious consequences.

"Tell me about these 'conflicts' as you call them, and with whom? What were the circumstances and the consequences or solution, if there was a solution at the time? Even the simplest thing you can think of might be a clue. Think of everything you remember, please."

Jennings hung his head.

Yes, he would have to admit that the organist at the church came to his mind first. Maureen and Kelli had always been at each other's throats, usually over the music at the church. Maureen would want a piece of music played one way and Kelli would want to play it another way, thinking it sounded better, more worshipful, perhaps, or the opposite was true.

Jennings had started to wonder if Maureen didn't pick on Kelli just because she thought she could in her position as music director and pastor's wife. Maureen always thought she was in a place of special honor in the church because of that, being the pastor's wife. Jennings had tried on several occasions to talk to her about it, but he had to approach the subject in such a way that Maureen would not be offended.

She always pretended she did not understand what he was talking about, but he always thought she knew exactly what he was saying. A pastor's wife was supposed to be humble, a person that served the members of the congregation, not expecting them to do her bidding. Jennings wasn't sure where, along the line, she had adopted the attitude that she was better than everyone else and hers was the only correct opinion.

He sighed.

"I was thinking of the church organist. Maureen and Kelli were always sniping at each other. It seems Maureen always wanted to find something wrong with Kelli's music, or her teaching, or something! But, like I said, I don't think Kelli would take it to the point of violence. She just seemed to take it! I always chalked it up as a personality conflict. You know what I mean by that."

Colton did know. In any group of people, there always seemed to be two that butted heads. There seemed to be one of those personality clashes at the office, between two of his officers. Something was going to have to be done about it. Colton had just not decided what yet.

So, yes, he nodded that he understood what that was about.

"They were both just Alpha females and unfortunately working at the same thing, in this case, the music for the church."

"Did one or the other ever threaten the other one in any way at all?" Colton asked.

"Oh, no, nothing like that, at least not that I knew of, and believe me, as pastor, you usually hear about everything that goes on in the church, by first one person and then another. It's usually one of one group of friends and another from another group, or clique, and yes, those exist in a church. In a way, the 'politics,' let's call it, in a church, are worse than on any other job."

Colton was not aware of that. Of course, he did not go to his church as often as some thought he should. The job just did not let him. A couple of times when he had decided to be a part of this group or that group, everyone was interrupted when his iPhone went off, with someone calling him in to work. This or that had happened that needed his attention. He would have to leave, disrupting further.

So, he had dropped out of everything at the church, except the occasional service. His wife was really the social mixer, anyway, and the church really gave her an outlet for all she wanted to do.

He was content to let her represent the family with her presence at things. Most understood his position, anyway, and made no judgments. But there were always a few with the barbed comments.

Yes, again, he understood what the pastor was saying.

"Anything or anyone else you can think of? Did she, or you, even, have any conflicts with anyone in the community?"

He based his question on what he had already learned from the second house down Dutch Mills South, sorry, State Line Road, which everyone he had talked to so far, still referred to the dirt, hard-packed road. If Mr. Frank admitted to the Carltons' son having several run-ins with the pastor's wife, then surely the pastor knew about them. You couldn't keep something like that quiet in a small community like this.

"I can't think right now," Jennings said. He put both hands on each side of his face, closing his eyes.

After several minutes, he continued.

"There were a couple of incidences with the son of the owner of the house just down the hill from the church and parsonage. The son is in his early twenties, something like that. He seems to really be a bum, but you really can't say that to anyone in the community, especially if you're trying to talk to them about attending church, which I tried to do several times. The man and his wife are really hermits. Actually, they keep to themselves even more than hermits, I think. His name is Henry Carlton, and he always referred to his wife as the missus, so I never knew her name. And that's been in the two years since we lived here.

"Anyway, the son comes and goes, and not very often, thank goodness, because you certainly can hear him when he comes. The radio on his truck is on so loud that the whole of Dutch Mills must surely be able to hear him, not to mention the people that live on the hill across from Dutch Mills on the highway. The bass is the worst part. The 'boom, boom,' of the bass just drives everyone up a wall. The only redeeming factor of the whole situation is that the son really doesn't come very often.

"One time was in the middle of the afternoon, last summer. Maureen was particularly tired from planting flowers and working in the garden for several days. She laid down for a nap and had just drifted off to sleep when you started to hear the bass of the man's radio as he turned into Dutch Mills off the highway. It became louder and louder, of course, as he drove into the community and stopped right down the hill. And he didn't turn the radio off when he got out of the pickup. The noise just went on and on.

"After a time, Maureen was so mad that she jumped out of bed, put on her shoes, and marched down the hill to their house. I could hear them arguing clear up at the house. That's how much voices carry here, especially in the afternoon when there is not much traffic or noise. Well, usually, of course.

"I heard a third voice, but could not hear what was said. But the music went off and, in a few minutes, Maureen came back into the house. She never got her rest, as you can imagine, and, unfortunately, I got the brunt of the whole situation all evening. I thought at the time that it was a good thing we didn't have a church service that evening, or the members might be sorry!"

The pastor stopped to take a breath. "It would actually be okay if she were here in the evenings to vent all her frustrations at me, now. What am I going to do without her?"

His voice caught in a sob.

Colton drove for several more miles before he asked another question.

"You said a couple of times. When was the other one?"

"Oh, months and months later. This time the young man came in the middle of the night, Saturday night. Same thing. Music too loud, not turning it off. Maureen went down there that time, too, but I went with her, since it was the middle of the night.

"She tried to explain to him that Sunday was our biggest working day and we needed to be able to sleep. He just laughed and said don't you mean that's your *only* working day? That's what a lot of people think, of course, that preachers, or preacher's wives only work on Sundays, but that really made her mad. She gave him a piece of her mind. But, with Mr. Carlton stepping in again, the music went off.

"But I knew by then that she had made an enemy of the young man, and perhaps the father, also. There was certainly no love lost between them from then on, between Maureen and the old man, I mean. Everyone knows you don't threaten the kids without the parents coming to the rescue. They might not like their children at all, but that doesn't mean someone outside the family can bully them. The old man told her in no uncertain terms that if Christians acted like her, he would certainly never step foot inside this church, or any other, for that matter."

Jennings sighed again.

"Sometimes, I'll have to admit, Maureen was not easy to get along with."

He gasped and looked over at Colton.

"Not with me, of course, it was just occasionally others would get on her nerves. "You don't think either of these situations would have been bad enough for either of them to consider killing her, do you? They were just arguments. People get into arguments all the time."

"We really do not know what to think yet, Pastor," Colton said. "We are still just asking questions and trying to piece all clues together. Unfortunately, the Carltons have been gone all this week, since the morning of the murder, in fact, and we have not been able to contact them or find out how to contact the son."

"I heard the man next down from them takes care of their cattle, chickens, and feeds the dogs when they go away. Did he have any contact information?"

"No, nothing. He had just been asked if he would look after the place. We've already talked to him and he says Henry Carlton never says where they are going or gives an emergency number, or anything," Colton said.

"By what I've heard of him, that's just like him," Jennings agreed.

Several more minutes went by. Eric had just kept quiet in the backseat, but Colton knew he had taken notes of everything the pastor said.

"Nothing else? Anybody else?" Colton asked.

"Nothing. Not that I can think of right now. But, I'll be sure to call you, if I think of anything. If you think it might have been intentional murder, then I certainly want to know who did such a thing. Do you suspect the son?"

"We don't suspect anyone right now, it's like I said, and we are just looking into every angle."

By this time, they were nearing Dutch Mills. Jennings had certainly given them both something to think about, though.

Now, they just had to wait for the Carltons to return. In the meantime, the interviews and vacuums would go on, with all three teams.

Chapter 19

For the next two weeks, for Colton and Eric, between everything else to do with the Sheriff's Department, their time was taken up with interviewing the owners of the houses down Dutch Mills South, sorry, State Line Road.

Although there was not a course a person could take to learn when a person was lying, no Lie Detection 101, or anything like that, no degree or certification to earn in that field, Colton had been trained to detect micro-expressions on people's faces. The expression would only last for a flash of a second before it was gone.

This micro-expression was more of a "tell" on the person. They were never aware that it had occurred. Only certain people had the ability to detect these. Some people, of course, could look you straight in the eye and tell a lie as big as the State of Texas and you would never be the wiser. Most people, though, had some sort of "tell." This might be in the form of a repeated gesture, a tic, a swallow, any number of things that the person did subconsciously without realizing it was happening.

Most of the homeowners down State Line Road (Colton realized they had started calling this road that, because all the people living on it did) were telling the truth about where they were the morning of the murder. Most were simply sleeping in their beds until the time they regularly got up. Some, of course, were disturbed by the storm, but were still at home.

No, they didn't see or hear anything strange or different down the road.

Colton and Eric had been warned that when they reached the south end of this road, you would be right on the Oklahoma line. If you strayed five feet to the west of the road, you would be in Oklahoma. That would have been a nightmare for the people here, because, since it was still in Arkansas, the Washington County Commissioner sent the road grader down the road on a regular basis, especially after a rain, to clear the road of all debris.

The road ended at South Arkansas Highway 244, which would end a few feet west and become Oklahoma Highway 51. They turned left, or east (you can't go straight). There were only three houses on this almost one mile stretch that was South Arkansas Highway 244.

They turned south into the first driveway they came to. A barking dog greeted them, but the owner soon quieted it.

Yes, he was expecting them at some point, he just didn't know when they would make it to his house.

"How far are you going to the south, anyway? A few more miles, just past Evansville, you'll be in Crawford County."

Colton told him they would check persons and vehicles in and around Evansville and that would be all for them, while other teams were elsewhere.

This man had most definite opinions on most things and kept them longer than they had hoped to be. He wanted to be indignant that they wanted to vacuum his pickup and car, but they knew he could not refuse the warrant. The other two places on this short stretch of highway would have to wait for another day.

It was not to be the next day, however, as a small incident kept Colton busy all day. That evening he received a call from Herman Frank saying that the Carltons had returned home from their trip, just that evening.

They would be there bright and early in the morning.

Chapter 20

Colton knew he could not let himself get tired of driving to Dutch Mills just about every other day, or every third day, at least. He felt sorry for all the people who drove from here day after day to work in Fayetteville or points further. They would have the morning sun in their eyes in the morning and be facing into the evening sun going home around 5:15, after getting off work at 5:00, and out of the city traffic. Many people did.

To each his own, though.

The Carltons had returned home fifteen days after being gone. They were surprised to see the Washington County Sheriff's cruiser pull into their driveway early the next morning. He just caught them, however, because they were going to buy groceries. Another fifteen minutes and he would have missed them.

Carlton had not heard about the murder of the pastor's wife early on the morning they had left for his sister-in-law's place near Gilbert, on the Buffalo River. It was a vacation spot for all of them, without TV or internet. They just enjoyed talking and mostly fishing. The women brought their yarn for crocheting, and knitting, and seemed content to talk, take walks, and cook the fish the men brought home. The cares of the world were left behind for those two plus weeks, two or three times a year.

The mosquitos had been pretty bad this year, though, Carlton was quick to inform them. They just didn't seem to ever take a vacation.

"We need to ask you some questions dealing with this situation," Colton began.

"We weren't here. How could we possibly help you?" Henry asked.

"It seems the murder must have taken place just about the time you left," Colton said.

The man went on the defensive.

"Are you accusing me or my wife of having something to do with it? We didn't have anything to do with it. We had this trip planned for at least a month before, to leave exactly at the time we did."

"Who did you tell about going on this trip?" Colton asked.

"Well, no one, I guess. Wasn't anyone else's business, don't you know. Herman down the next place helps me with the animals while we're gone, has for years now. But he never asks where we are going, and we never tell him."

"It must just be coincidence that you left at about the same time. Can you think of anything you might have seen or heard out of the ordinary?"

"It was raining cats and dogs. What kind of weather do we get, when we get a hurricane in Arkansas? Didn't think I would ever be in one of those. We figured, going east, that we would drive out of it, which we did. By the time we reached the river, the storm was going back west, or so the radio said."

"Please, Mr. Carlton, think about it. Even the smallest detail might be important, something you might not even consider important."

"Oh, oh, I forgot just then, but now, come to think of it, there was this little car parked down at the end of the road there." He pointed down the road toward the community, to the end of his property.

"It was parked just at the corner fence post there. 'Course, I couldn't see much because of the growth on my fence down this side. Keep telling myself I'm going to take all that off, just don't seem to get around to it. I'm not lazy, now don't you think that, it's just there always seems to be something else to do. Anyway, I couldn't really see it for the hard rain and overgrowth."

"Then, how did you know there was even a car there?" Colton inquired. He felt Eric getting as excited as he was. This was more information, a lead, a *clue*, in this case. Surely it would be important.

"It looked like the headlights went on, then off again, then on again. It didn't move, though. Just sat there. I couldn't tell if someone got out or got in, or if anyone was still in it. I saw some lights flickering through the trees, so I thought perhaps it had gone and I couldn't see, but when we left, we passed it. Still sitting there. Dark.

"Then, I thought I saw more lights, but I guess it was just reflections of the lightning or something."

Again, he pointed to the house, the only house on the small stretch of road, of a few hundred yards, that took you into Dutch Mills off the highway. Then, you had to turn either right or left (you can't go straight).

"Then, I thought I saw lights again flickering in the trees going south on Highway 59. Couldn't tell you if it was the same vehicle, though. That car might have turned north and the one I saw just another one traveling south. The timing was right, though. There was just too much rain to see much of anything. Wondered about all that traffic in that weather. About that time, we got in the pickup and started on our trip. I told you it was raining hard, didn't I?"

"Yes, yes, you did," Colton responded. He had to keep his voice steady. It wouldn't do for this man to think they thought he was the killer.

"That's when we saw it just sitting there."

"And your sister-in-law can verify when you arrived at their place?" Eric asked.

"Well, yeah, sure, but we also stopped to eat on the way, at Alpena, like we always do. There was a new place there. The café we had ate at for many years had gone out of business. Not too many travelers that way, I guess, especially now that they put in the new Highway 412. Probably closed up a lot of businesses. It even bypasses Huntsville, and that must have hurt them there. Is that progress? Just because people want to get to Branson faster, to start having fun. Businesses closing are people's lives."

Colton ignored that.

"Can you give us her phone number?"

"My sister? Well, sure, of course."

"Mr. Carlton, we also have a warrant granting us the right to search and vacuum your vehicles. Do you mind?"

"My pickup, you mean. I only own the one vehicle. But what do you need to do that for? Haven't even had a chance to bring in all the stuff from the trip."

"We don't mind that, and we can't discuss the reason we need to do this, but we appreciate your cooperation."

Eric got busy with the bags and vacuum cleaner. He thoroughly vacuumed the luggage and bags from the trip.

Colton continued his conversation with Henry.

"I've been told that your son came to your home about that time, also. You must have just missed him by a few minutes."

"My son?"

Carlton looked startled. It appeared to Colton to be genuine surprise.

"I didn't know he was coming that day, or that morning. 'Course, he never calls or tells me he's coming, or when he's coming back the next time. Don't think he knows. Just comes here to crash sometimes. Sorry, Sheriff, but some- times he gets drunk and seems to think our place is the best place to sleep it off. We have a small bedroom round the back of the house. He has a key to the backdoor. All he has to do is unlock the door, step inside a few feet, and he's there.

"We've got up sometimes and he's here. We've de- cided we have to do something about the boy, but haven't decided what yet. Coming on in while we're gone is just too much, though. I bet Herman, just down the road told you, didn't he?"

"Yes, he did," Colton admitted. "He saw the pickup here when he came to milk your cow and feed. While he was milking, he heard your son come out and drive away. He didn't know what time he got here, though."

"Had to have been after 4:00 a.m., 'cause that's when we left."

Just about the right time, Colton thought. *Roy put the time of death at around 4:00 a.m. I wonder if this man has starting thinking that it looks like either one of them could have done it. Maybe they did it together.*

"Tell us your son's name and where he lives. We want to talk with him. And, please, don't call and tell him we're coming. We would like to find him at home."

"Don't worry. I won't call him. If he's gotten himself into any kind of trouble, then he'll just have to get himself out. He won't get any help from me."

And I wonder why he is like he is, Colton thought, *with all this love and support!*

They left.

Next stop, the small community of Greenland, south of Fayetteville.

Chapter 21

Unfortunately, the days of the investigation about the murder seemed to go by in some sort of routine. Each of the two-person teams seemed to only be able to interview two homeowners per day, and some days not even two. Not all the teams were available all the time for the investigation.

There really were the usual day-to-day minor and a few major incidents that needed the attention of a sheriff's department, as opposed to a city police department. Anything that happened in the county had to be investigated.

There was a big to-do when a wealthy cattle farmer had some of his prize steers stolen. Wondering at the time where you hid about 50 head of cattle, they were all eventually found, one and two at a time. They had been stolen when the farmer was away and the farmhand had gone to his own home for a night, although he was supposed to stay at the big farm.

That made it seem like an inside job, because who else would know when he was gone?

It turned out that four men had been watching for just such an opportunity. What it boiled down to, though, was that all the time spent on incidents like that took away from the murder investigation.

They drove slowly into Greenland, a small community situated about three miles south of Fayetteville, still in Washington County.

That was good. That made this visit all the better. There was no other sheriff to notify of what they were doing there and the reason. This was Colton's jurisdiction.

Drake Field, now an executive airport since the Northwest Regional Airport was built in Highfill, Arkansas, seventeen miles west of Fayetteville, was just a stone's throw away. They would probably go back into Fayetteville by this route. There were a couple of small communities south of Fayetteville, now off exits of Interstate 71.

Greenland was no exception. As they entered the city on Highway 265, on the western edge of the city, they saw it was also called Razorback Road. This road could take you directly to the main entrance of the University of Arkansas.

Henry Carlton had given them the address where his son was staying. Colton thought that had been a strange choice of wording. Carlton had not said 'living,' just 'staying.'

Using their GPS, they were approaching the location. This was definitely the not-so-wealthy part of town, which there actually seemed to be little of. This small community seemed to be a quiet, family-oriented community.

Colton thought this might be an ideal spot to live. You were in a small, almost country setting, yet just minutes away from the bigger city, the University of Arkansas for a sport enthusiast, and an airport, which actually could connect you to a larger airport, then anywhere you might want to go.

They had passed a city park with modern playground equipment and an impressive water park.

Family and children friendly.

As with all communities, large or small, there were always those 'haves' and 'have-nots,' often located in the same subdivision, but mostly in different areas of the community.

They pulled up in front of a house that could have used some TLC. Paint was peeling off the front porch columns and the yard had seen its better days in the way of care and maintenance. The larger area had been mowed, but somebody sure could have used a weed eater around the edge of the house and porch. There may have been a flower bed at one time, but not now.

Looking up and down the street, there were one or two more in ill repair, but this was definitely the worst one.

Colton looked over at Eric.

"Flop house?" Colton asked.

"Could be, we'll just have to wait and see," Eric responded.

They quietly and cautiously walked up the front steps to the screened-in front door.

There was no doorbell, so they knocked as loudly as they could on the doorframe. They could hear loud music in the house.

They again looked at each other. That made sense, since that seemed to be the complaint from the pastor's wife that had caused her confrontations with this young man.

The door was open a crack.

They opened the screen door and gently and slowly pushed open the wooden frame door. They both took a couple of steps into the living room. They were just ready to call out and identify themselves when a young man stepped out of the first door to the right down the hall.

He pointed a shotgun at them. He looked surprised to see the uniforms but continued pointing the gun at them.

"Whoa," he said. "What are you doing here, walking into someone's house without announcing yourself?"

Both men had put their hands up. Their training taught them that, when looking down the barrel of a gun, you keep all hands in sight.

They faced a young man in his late teens, possibly early twenties, but no more. His hair was uncombed, probably 'bedhead' and he looked as if he had slept in the same clothes he had on right now. The T-shirt was stained in the front. By the odor, they both knew he had not showered in a couple of days. He had not shaved for several days by the growth of the stubble on his chin.

Not-so-focused eyes stared at them. Maybe he hadn't even comprehended that he was pointing a lethal weapon at two uniformed police officers.

Colton answered. "We did knock, as loud as we could. You probably didn't hear because of the loud music."

"Mister, you need to consider what you are doing here," Colton continued. "You are holding a gun on two uniformed police officers, which is a crime, in fact, it's a felony. You need to put the gun down, and quickly."

The gun stayed up and in place.

Hands stayed up and in place.

"Mister, put the gun down," Colton repeated. He was now starting to use his 'police' voice, a harder, more demanding tone than he usually took with people. This tone usually had the desired effect.

Still the gun stayed up and in place.

"Put the gun down, Ralph," said a voice behind the young man. Ralph hesitated a second or two more, then moved aside, placing the shotgun on a table next to the hall.

Colton and Eric slowly lowered their hands.

They were now facing another young man, but several years older than the first one. His eyes were harder, for one thing. This young man had already been rode hard and put up wet, more times than a young man of his age should have been.

Was this the fault of the father, Henry Carlton, that this young man looks like this and probably knows more about life than he should at this young age? thought Colton. In their interview with Henry Carlton, they had definitely sensed there was no love lost between father and son. Carlton had probably been a hard taskmaster as the young boy grew into a hard young man, full of resentment, and possibly rage.

There were signs around his eyes, mouth and a general appearance that this young man was an alcoholic in the making, if not a full-blown one already.

Where do they get the money for all that liquor? I've always wondered that, Colton thought, again. *Is this young man dealing?*

This was just a split-second assessment of the young man by Colton, and he admitted to himself just now, that he was not a psychiatrist, just judging from his law enforcement experience. He really hoped he was wrong.

"Help you, gentlemen?" the other young man asked.

"You can, and now Ralph, is it, is in trouble. Pointing a weapon at a police officer is against the law. But I suspect you know that, don't you?"

He continued, "We are looking for Ricky Carlton. His dad said we could find him here, that he stayed here."

There was a hesitation, as if this second young man was deciding whether or not to tell them where Ricky was.

Finally, although it was only a second in reality, the young man made up his mind.

"I'm Ricky Carlton," he said. "And Ralph here didn't mean any harm with the shotgun. I don't even think it's loaded. He didn't know who you were when he stepped out of the kitchen."

I bet it is, and he knew who we were as he continued holding up the gun, Colton thought. *Ricky is just concerned for his friend. He knows he just committed a crime and hopes we'll overlook it.*

"Yet he didn't put the gun down when we told him to," Colton argued. He wasn't going to let him off the hook. "But we'll get back to the gun later."

It was time to introduce themselves.

"I am Washington County Sheriff Colton Mitchell, and this is Chief Deputy Eric Simmons. We've come here to talk to you, Ricky, concerning an investigation we have ongoing. Just a few questions. Ralph, stay put. Don't go anywhere," Colton said, again in his police voice.

This latter part he directed toward Ralph, who had turned to go back down the hall. He turned back when the sheriff addressed him. He looked at Ricky, seemingly for permission to stay or go.

"Don't look at Ricky for permission to move," Colton said, "you do as I tell you."

"Take a seat, Ralph," Colton ordered, pointing to a chair.

Ralph did. His dominance with the shot gun was now over.

"Why don't we sit down, Ricky?"

"Sure," came the reply.

Colton and Eric quickly glanced around. Since some of the furniture seemed questionable, Colton chose to put a leg up on an overstuffed chair arm, with the other leg straight, making him standing and sitting at the same time, yet in a seemingly casual way. There was nothing casual about their positions, though, and Colton figured Ricky knew this.

"What's going on?" Ricky asked. "I can assure you I, we," he motioned toward Ralph, "have done nothing wrong, well, besides this gun business, of course."

Some incidents must have been their fault, in the past, for him to say that, Colton thought.

"We just have a few questions, for both of you."

An unspoken 'now' was in the air, in light of the shotgun pointed at them a few minutes before.

Colton directed his first question to Ricky. They all noticed that Eric had taken out a notebook and pen. This would be recorded. Ricky understood the significance of that.

"So, where were you the night of Thursday, June 3rd, and the morning of Friday, June 4th, a little over two weeks ago?"

The two young men looked at each other.

"We both were having a few drinks out to The Oasis. You know that nightclub between Fayetteville and Farmington, on Highway 62 West."

"I hope that means that Ralph, here, is at least twenty-one years of age."

Colton was looking at Ralph. He saw panic in his eyes.

"I…I'm *almost* twenty-one, Sheriff," he said. Again, he looked at Ricky.

It appeared that Ricky was going to be in trouble for contributing to the delinquency of a minor, which would include the bartender and owner of The Oasis, also.

They had definitely opened a can of worms here. Colton wondered how big the can was and how many worms would start wiggling out.

Ricky looked directly at the sheriff. How far was this sheriff willing to carry this knowledge, which he knew was going to be minor compared to whatever this investigation was. He knew that finding out all these little incidentals was not part of the sheriff's plan. Something bigger was going on here.

Colton was right to think this young man had seen more than his share of the wrong side of life. He had not served any time for a felony, just a few misdemeanors, drinking and carousing, mostly, fighting with other bar patrons, that sort of thing. Those were in his minor days, so nothing was on his record.

But still too many things as a youth.

It brought on a certain cynicism and hardness in one's life that should not be there in a person this age.

But that was his life and he played his cards as they had been dealt to him.

"What did you drink? Just you, right now, Ricky," Colton asked.

"Let me think."

Ricky blinked a couple of times. Colton could well believe that it was probably hard for him to remember fifteen days ago. There was no telling how much liquor he had consumed since then.

"I had a few beers, then a few Jack Daniels, then some more beer."

He gestured with his right hand, as if in dismissal.

"I really can't remember how many in all," he concluded. "But I am twenty-four, so that was legal."

Colton nodded. He noted that Ricky had said "I" this time, instead of we.

"And you, Ralph?"

He looked over at Ralph, who had calmed down a little, but not much. He was more concerned for Ricky, who had taken him to The Oasis, than for himself. He might get a misdemeanor charge and have to pay a fine, which money he did not have, but his friend could do jail time. He couldn't remember if that was a felony, or not.

He jumped, startled, when the sheriff asked him the question.

"I...I had a few beers, maybe one whiskey. I don't remember how many beers," he answered, just barely above a whisper. But the two officers heard the answer. They knew he knew he was in trouble. Unlike Ricky, he hadn't been around long enough to realize there was something bigger here.

"And when did you leave? Together? Separately?" Colton directed the question back to Ricky.

"About 2:30 a.m. I remember it was that late because Matt, the bartender, had locked the door to any outside traffic, but he usually let the ones that were there, stay for a while. He wouldn't serve anymore liquor or beer, though, after 2:00. He's a real stickler for the law in that way, as is the owner of the place, Jack. The owner was still there, at a table in the corner, after closing. He could vouch for us until that time, if that's what you need. At 2:30 they told us to go. They always ask anyone still there if they are able to drive, or do they need to call a friend, or something. They really seem concerned that way."

Sure they are, Colton thought. *They are just making sure they cover their asses within the law. They are not supposed to let anyone leave and drive that appears to be too drunk to do so. But I wonder how many they don't care about, one way or the other. Boy, I must be tired. I am really being judgmental today.*

"But we assured them we could drive. Ralph had come in his own car because we sometimes leave at different times. That night we just happened to come separately. I mean, as opposed to coming together, which we do at times."

Ricky ran his fingers through his hair, which had been pretty disheveled to begin with. Now it was sticking up.

"Ralph turned back this way, to go home, here, I suppose." They all looked at Ralph, who nodded.

"I came straight here and fell into bed. Didn't wake up until noon."

Colton nodded. Ralph was not the one he was concerned with.

Ricky knew he was the one being questioned, simply because his father had directed the sheriff here. He wondered what was going on, but decided to wait until the sheriff said something, if he did. He would question his father later, when he yelled at him about revealing his location.

"And you went where?"

Again, Colton directed the question to Ricky.

Man, this guy won't let up! Ricky thought. *I wonder why it's so important where I went?*

But he answered the question.

"I didn't want to come back here," he gestured around the living room. "This place becomes a real drag sometimes. Sorry about that, Ralph, but you know how it is."

He directed this last statement at his friend.

Ralph nodded. He lowered his head.

"I decided to go to my folks' place, in Dutch Mills and crash there. That's a small community over on Highway 59, south of Lincoln." He looked from one to the other.

They nodded their understanding of where Dutch Mills was.

"They weren't there, which surprised me, since it was around 4:00 before I got there. I didn't drive so fast and I took the cutoff before you go into Lincoln, the highway down through Cane Hill. It's usually the way I take to get to Dutch Mills and I thought I might not face so much traffic that way."

As drunk as you probably were, what you mean is, you thought you might not run into the local Lincoln police officer, Kenny, on night duty, Colton thought.

"The only thing I could think of why they were not at home was one of their trips to the Buffalo River to visit with mom's sister and her husband. But, that didn't matter. I have a key to the back door. I let myself in. There's a small bedroom off the kitchen, just to the right of the backdoor. I crashed on the bed. I woke up a few hours after that and decided I might as well head back here. If mom wasn't there to cook a good breakfast for me and make a big pot of strong coffee to help get me on my feet, there wasn't any reason to stay there.

"I left there around 6:00 and came straight here. Ralph was still in bed. I went back to bed, myself, in my room. Then I woke up about 3:00. Felt like crap."

"Is there anyone to verify that you were at your folks' place at those times?"

"I don't know." Ricky shrugged. "I have no idea who might have driven past on State Line Road while my pickup was there."

"Did you see anyone or anything else, anything maybe out of the ordinary that might have caught your attention?"

"No, sir, it was really hard to see, that's another reason I was driving so slowly and it took me so long to get to Dutch Mills. It was really raining cats and dogs. No, wait a minute. I *did* see another vehicle. It was a small car. It was parked just at the corner of dad's property as you turned the corner left onto State Line Road, right where the drive comes down from the church. I almost hit it, not expecting anything to be there. I mean, there never is anything parked there.

"Someone must have had a flat or something, or just waiting out the worst of the storm, because it was pretty bad right then. Those were my two thoughts about it. I've been known to pull over to the side of the highway when it was bad like this. It's just too difficult to see what's coming, or even if you are in your own lane, or anything. The car wasn't there when I left in the morning, but the storm had let up a lot."

All this information collaborated with what Henry Carlton had said. The small whitish car parked on the corner facing south. Raining cats and dogs with hardly any visibility.

"You didn't think it was strange that your folks would leave in that sort of weather?"

Ricky laughed. "Hell, no, dad would not have changed his plans for anybody or anything. He's just that stubborn. So, if he told you I lived here, they must be home, right? They never call me to tell me when they are home or when they are going somewhere. Just like that night, I might travel all the way out there, and no one will be home. I've waited around several hours before, ate some leftovers, mom makes the best fried chicken, and the cold chicken is even better that when it's first cooked, at least in my opinion, but gave up and came home before they return. They'll probably be dead and rotting in the bed before anyone knows they are. Besides, dad and I argued the last time I was there, so he's for sure not going to tell me their plans."

He sounded somewhat bitter. Colton felt that deep down, the young man probably wanted to be in his parents' lives more, but the dad kept him away. He wasn't about to tell Ricky that the locks were getting changed and he wouldn't even have the opportunity to unexpectedly show up and get into the house.

At least this explained to Colton why Mr. Carlton planned to change the locks. The young man was probably so much like the dad, they had butted heads for years now, with neither of them willing to give in to the other, over anything.

"Did you hear or see anything else besides the car parked on the corner? Any unusual noises?"

"No, but the thunder would not have helped that. It sounded like it was right over head. Once a bolt of lightning seemed to strike the house, but I guess not. Well, yes, sorry, there were a couple of vehicles on Highway 59 just as I turned onto it, after waiting a few minutes for the rain to let up. Couldn't tell much about them in the storm, and all. Made me wonder, though, why anyone would be out in rain like that if he didn't have to."

Like you? Colton thought. He didn't say it, of course.

The car on the corner and a vehicle at the junction were the two things that jelled with the dad's story. They probably belonged to each other. Colton wondered if the young man really didn't hear anything at Dutch Mills.

"But, can I ask why you are asking me this?" Ricky asked. "It seems to be such strange questions."

"You haven't heard what happened that night, or should I say, around 4:00 that Friday morning, in Dutch Mills?"

Ricky looked blank, shaking his head no. Ralph was waiting for the answer, also.

There was no tell-tell micro-expressions on either of their faces. They were actually waiting for his answer.

Instead, he looked around, then asked another question.

"No TV?" he asked.

Ricky managed to look sheepish.

"It was repossessed about three weeks ago for non-payment." He looked over at Ralph. "Ralph was in charge of the payments for that, but he lost his last job and didn't tell anyone. The first I heard of it, two men were here to take the TV. They wouldn't even let me make up the payments. Said it was too late for that. We haven't replaced the set since."

Colton had noticed an iPhone sitting on the coffee table, though. It was the latest version, and he knew the cost of those, plus the cost of the data plan, monthly fees, etc. And going over the set amount of data could really rack up the charges. Yet that hadn't been repossessed.

Colton pointed at it. He spoke to Ricky.

"That your phone?"

"Yes, sir, it is,"

"Does it work?"

"Yes, sir, it does." Ricky answered.

"It hasn't been repossessed, I see," Colton countered.

"No, sir."

"Do you get any of the local TV news channels on it?"

"Well, I suppose I could, if I really wanted to. Don't usually care to, though. News is really not my thing. Seems it's just who murdered who and where, or which city had the latest terrorist attack. I have enough trouble just living without hearing all that all the time."

Colton could actually relate to that. It was just about what his wife said.

"So, what have you been doing with yourself for the last two weeks?"

"I've applied for some jobs, filling out the applications, and whatever. You have to be able to give them a phone number, so that's why I have the phone. Other than that, I've just hung around here, mostly, and back to The Oasis a couple of times. They can tell you that there."

"Oh, we'll ask, you can be sure of that," Colton replied.

"To answer your question, I am asking you all these questions because there was a murder in Dutch Mills around 4:00 a.m. that Friday morning, about the same time your dad left and you arrived, then left. It could not have been more that several minutes one way or the other. Are you sure the car was the only thing you saw? No person or persons around?"

Both Ricky and Ralph had looked so surprised at this news that Colton knew for sure it was the first time they heard about it. Unless they read the *Northwest Arkansas Times* or *The Morning News*, and Colton saw no evidence of a newspaper at all around the room, then this might just possibly be the first time they heard of it. It was no longer news to the region, and was never on the front page when it had appeared as an article.

Ricky almost blanched at the news.

"Oh, hell," he said. "Oh, sorry, Sheriff, it's just sounds so unlikely for there. Who was it, anyway? I mean the person who was murdered. If you are questioning me, you must not have anyone in custody yet as a suspect."

Ricky's next reaction would tell Colton all he needed to know. Unless, of course, Ricky was one of those people who could look you right in the eye and lie with a straight face, no 'tells; at all.

"It was the pastor's wife, of the church on the hill. Maureen Murphy."

He watched Ricky closely. He could see when the information registered and what it would look like concerning him.

Ricky looked genuinely surprised. He recovered quickly.

"And you're questioning me because we've had a couple of run-ins. Even yelling matches. You think I might have killed her, don't you? But I didn't, honest. I usually totally forgot about the run-ins as soon as I drive away. I kind of thought they were funny, and she was a little wacko, if you know what I mean. It was just loud music. When did that ever hurt anyone? Honest, Sheriff, I never harmed the lady."

Colton could tell the way the young man talked that he was begging Colton to believe him. Ricky had already worked out the consequences for him, especially without an alibi and the murder taking place at the same time.

The small car on the corner may or may not have anything to do with anything. Just a coincidence.

Or, the father and son might have gotten together, made up the car to cover something up.

"I'm in trouble, aren't I?" he asked Colton.

"Right now, we are just asking questions. We have a warrant to search your vehicle and vacuum it. We might as well do that right now."

Colton and Eric stood up.

"Vacuum the pickup? That sounds like an odd thing to do. You won't find a gun or anything. I don't own one. This shotgun," Ricky gestured toward the shotgun Ralph had placed on the table. "This belonged to Ralph's grandpa and he gave it to Ralph before he passed away recently."

"Do you own a dog?" Colton asked.

"No," Ricky answered. "What's that got to do with anything?"

"We're looking for dog hairs."

"You're looking for dog hairs? What's that got to do with murdering the pastor's wife?"

"Just an angle we're pursuing," Colton answered, casually.

"Wait!" Ricky exclaimed. "She came down that afternoon when she chewed me out about my loud music with a little dog on a leash. It wouldn't stop barking, especially when dad's two dogs started barking at it."

"But I still don't see the connection," he finished. He was frowning. Then, he looked up at Colton. Colton almost saw the light bulb come on above his head.

"It was a robbery and the dog was killed to shut it up before Mrs. Murphy caught the burglar. That's it, isn't it?"

Colton and Eric both laughed.

"You could write good detective stories, it sounds like," Colton said.

"I'm right, I know I am. Why else would you be vacuuming vehicles? You might find some dog hairs from dad's one dog. The beagle always wants to jump up in the pickup whenever I open a door, from either side. But that's the only dog hairs you should find in there."

"We'll see," Colton responded. "Thank you for your time, both of you. Please do not plan to leave town. We might need to question each of you further."

He looked over at the younger man.

"And, Ralph, I'm going to overlook the fact that you held a gun on an officer of the law, only because we have more pressing business to take care of than running you in. But, know this, if your name appears before me for even the slightest thing, we won't forget this, get it?"

Colton's tone was enough to scare anyone.

"Yes, sir, I got it," the young man responded.

"And be here," Colton said to both of them. He looked from first one to the other.

"Only plan on going to work somewhere," Ricky answered.

He watched as the cruiser drove away.

Someone killed the pastor's wife!

Chapter 22

s they drove away, Colton and Eric spoke at the same time.

"What do you think?" Colton asked. Colton's opinion would be the one that counted, although he always listened and checked out all opinions.

"He seems like the usual suspect to me."

Colton answered the question with a question of his own.

"Coincidence, you think? Could the killer's car be in the same place, or close enough for government work, at the same time Henry and Mae Carlton left town at the same time, and, in enough time to have sideswiped each other, the son showed up at the house? What are the odds on all three of those things happening at the same time? We'll have to check all this out further, of course.

"But you have to admit this is the closest we have come to the killer. Don't you think?"

"I do," Eric admitted. "I'm not sure I believe in coincidences. This is not our first rodeo when it comes to things like this. It's just too convenient."

"Maybe too convenient," Colton responded. "We'll have to think about this, put it all together. Then, we'll plan our next move with the Carltons.

"Let's drop this bag off at the lab and go home for the day. When he mentioned fried chicken, I realized how hungry I was. It's been a busy day."

"You can say that again," Eric agreed.

Chapter 23

Here they were, back where Colton had left off when he first explored this county after moving here.

Here was the same name on the same rusty mailbox on the same weathered wooden post.

The name on the mailbox read "Hat aba gh."

This was the last "pig-trail" he had found on the 911 map, but did not go down the further, less traveled trail, which had to end at a house somewhere further in these woods. He felt he only made it this far because the rural mail carrier had to come this way when this person had mail, which meant the carrier also had to bring third- and fourth- class mail down here.

At the time, he told himself he would only go further if he needed to, if it were absolutely necessary.

Now, it had become absolutely necessary.

He was tempted to skip this place. It was almost to the Crawford County line, the county just south of Washington, totally in the boonies. But, if he didn't go to the house, or whatever he might find further, he would always regret it. He had promised that he would leave no stone unturned in this investigation, so here he was. He thought if he went slowly enough, the Range Rover should be okay.

But maybe he should just leave it here, right? At least he knew he could turn around here. What if he couldn't further on? Backing out was not an option.

They got out and locked the car. At least the hand-held vacuum was not heavy. Their biggest worry was dogs.

Loose dogs, as in no-chained-up or fenced-in dogs.

He really didn't believe a dog, or any animal, should be chained up, that was simply against the animal's nature and he considered it unnecessarily cruel. What if a couple of stray dogs came up the chained-up dog and decided to attack it? The dog would be defenseless and would probably die a horrible death at the 'hands' of the other dogs. Too much for him to think about. But, he had to admit, he had been glad on occasions that a dog had been chained up.

"There's a cattle guard," Colton observed.

"That's what it's called," Eric agreed.

"I didn't see this the first time I was here. I stopped a little way back, before the mailbox. I haven't seen one in a long time."

"Yep, they still make them. All my uncles have them at their farms, here in Washington County. Didn't they have them in Marion County?" Eric asked.

"Oh, yeah, I just never asked why a person used one. Instead of a regular gate, that is."

"Well," Eric said, "I'm not so sure the person uses it, or doesn't use it, as much as the cattle don't use it. It keeps them inside the pasture most effectively. Some people think cows are stupid, but they aren't. They are really very intelligent. They might think, from a distance, they can get out this way, to the grass that is always greener looking on the other side, in the other pasture, but when they get here, they stop. They have enough sense to know they can't cross this with their hooves. Any hoofed animal that is kept behind here cannot cross this and they know it."

"Is it cheaper than a regular gate?" Colton asked. He would have to admit that he was not farmer-savvy.

"I don't think so. I think they cost much more, because they are so much more convenient. Keeps the owners' animals in, others out, and the owners dry. In rainy weather, if you come and go through here very much, you don't have to stop your vehicle, get out, open the gate, get back in the vehicle, drive through, stop the vehicle, get out and close the gate, then back to the vehicle to continue. All this time getting soaking wet, of course, or cold, or whatever. This way, you can get in the vehicle under your carport or from your garage and never have to stop like I said. You pay for that convenience, but it's worth it."

"Of course," Colton returned. "It doesn't look like this one was been used in a long time, by the looks of the overgrown field here."

"I don't think so, either," Eric answered. "It's at least as old as we are, if not older, but they never wear out."

"Well, let's take ourselves across," Colton said.

He found a good sturdy stick, just the right size. He could use it to walk with, but it might deter a dog, dogs, until the owner came.

It was at least three quarters of a mile down the trail before they saw a roof of some sorts. It had different color shingles on it, but maybe it kept the rain out.

They stopped in full view of the house. It was in pretty decent shape, actually, considering where it was. There was a small, older type pickup in the yard. Colton wondered if that vehicle could actually negotiate the trail. It was certainly small enough, but he would question its sturdiness. There was also a Toyota Corolla. Colton couldn't ever tell what year those were, but it was not a new one. It was a light color, dirty license plate.

"Hello, the house!" he called as loudly as he could.

They knew better than to go right up to the door. Even now, a shotgun might appear out a window. Some of the windows did not appear to have screens on them, but that might be the lighting through the trees. It was a bright, sunny day.

Cool, but bright. Autumn was definitely in the air, but they might have an Indian summer.

The front door opened, and a man stepped out. When he saw the uniforms, he turned back and to the right. Colton knew he must have leaned a shotgun back inside.

"Howdy, Sheriff," the man said. "Come on up to the porch and sit a spell. That be quite a walk from the mailbox, ain't it? What brings you all the way to my humble abode. I promise I ain't done nothing wrong, at least not lately. Gettin' too old to cut the mustard, you know."

He laughed at his own joke.

Colton and Eric walked toward the house when the man invited them. Colton felt no malice in the man. He was probably just a hermit, liked to live way out by himself.

"I'm Colton Mitchell, the sheriff of Washington County and this is my deputy, Eric. And you are?" Colton left the question open-ended. He would see if this man was the same as the name on the mailbox. If not, that presented a whole list of other questions.

"Name's Van Hattabaugh," he answered. "Live here by myself, so you don't have to worry about anyone else. Don't get too many visitors, either."

"No dogs?" Colton asked. Usually people in the country like this had a least one dog, if not more.

"Old Yeller died awhile back, and I haven't had the heart to replace him yet," was the response. "Thought I might pick up two next time, though. It seemed like Old Yeller was lonely at times. I was just thinking of going into town, to the pound, in the next day or two and see what they got.

"But I bet that's not what you're here for. I mean, you're not collecting for a cause, are you? I seem to be my own charity here." He gestured toward the yard.

He laughed, again.

"No, sir, that's not the reason we are here. We are investigating a murder that took place in Dutch Mills about six weeks ago."

"Whew!" the man responded. "Yeah, I heard about that. The pastor's wife, right? I don't go to church anywhere but can't see why anyone would want to kill a preacher's wife, even if it weren't the same religion and all that. What's the good in that? I'm sure she was just minding her own business, as she sees it."

Colton was not so sure of that, by what he had heard from various people, but this man would never know that.

"I heard it might have a burglar, a robbery gone wrong, the robber caught in the act and all that, so he shot her before she could scream or anything," the man offered.

If he hoped that Colton or Eric would supply any information, he was wrong.

"There certainly have been many theories going around, we know that. We can't comment, of course. Our investigation isn't finished yet. Can you tell us where you were the night of Thursday, June 2nd and morning of Friday, June 3rd?"

"Right here, of course, don't get out much, as I said. But, there's no one to prove that, so it's just my word you have to go on. Didn't kill her, though."

Colton doubted that he had, he just had to ask all the questions.

Anyway, who was going to admit it if they did?

He held out the warrant to the man. "We have a warrant to search and vacuum your vehicles, sir. Do you mind?"

The man laughed. "Now, what good would it do if I did mind? Go ahead, whatever you need to do."

Mr. Hattabaugh appeared surprised, though, when they held up the vacuum. They had to clean some papers and other trash out of the car, vacuuming each item, before they got to the floorboards and between the seats and console. They were very thorough, though. The man took the trash from them when they were finished.

As rough as his house and yard seemed, he appeared to be embarrassed that the car was so messed up.

"My wife used to keep the vehicle spotless," he said. He sounded almost apologetic. "Since she's been gone, I don't seem to have a will to do it."

"I understand," Colton replied. "It's hard to lose your spouse."

"Yeah, after forty-five years, it was. Don't have a heart to keep much picked up since she's been gone." Again, he gestured around the yard.

It didn't take long to vacuum the pickup. Of the two vehicles, it had less in it than the car.

Colton and Lane were finished. They would hand the bag over to the forensics team, as all the other bags from all the other deputies had been given to the lab. He wasn't expecting much from these bags.

His "hair-brained theory," as he knew the men called it, was not yet producing any results. The lab made regular reports. He was sure they would only find hairs from this man's dog that had recently died.

They thanked him. Mr. Hattabaugh offered to drive them back to their car, but they declined, saying the exercise would do them good.

"Well, that's it with all the places this far out," Colton began, as they walked along. "Just a few more interviews and vacuum jobs. At least I'll know I checked everything."

"And no one can fault you on that," Eric agreed.

They were both keenly aware of how long it had been and still there was no suspect, much less a culprit and arrest.

The whole department was feeling the pressure, but no one more so than Colton.

Chapter 24

When she opened her front door a crack, she saw two uniformed officers.

"Yes?" she asked.

"Excuse us, ma'am, I am Washington County Sheriff Colton Mitchell and this is my partner, Chief Deputy Eric Simmons. May we ask you some questions pertaining to an investigation?"

She still had not opened the door any wider. She could not see a patrol car because of the way the door was recessed in relation to the garage and the driveway.

"May I see some identification?" she asked.

"Of course," Colton responded. They both brought out their badges and ID cards and held them up so she could see.

"Okay, I know your names. What are your badge numbers?"

What is this? Colton wondered. *I can appreciate a single woman living alone wanting to see some identification, but this is beyond.*

After they had said their numbers, she responded, "Just a minute. Don't go away."

They looked at each other and shrugged. What was going on?

Karen quickly looked up the number for the Washington County Sheriff's Office, called it and verified the names and numbers. She asked the lady on the line to describe the two men, and she did an excellent job.

Karen picked up her house keys.

She quickly opened the door, unlocked the storm door, and stepped out onto the stoop as the two men backed up. They had no choice.

She pulled the door shut and it locked behind her. She did not want the men in her home.

"Right, officers. Now, what can I do for you?"

"As we said, we are conducting an investigation, a murder investigation, to be exact. You may have heard of it. The pastor's wife at the little church at Dutch Mills, about thirty miles south of here, was killed about two months ago. We are talking to everyone involved with the church. It is our understanding that you and your husband were members there."

"No, we were never members there, but we did attend when we lived there for a while. But it's been at least a year and a half since we've been there. We moved up here about two years ago, and visited down there every once in a while for a while, then quit making that drive. That was after my mother passed away. Sadly, my husband passed away six months ago. But I still attend the Bible Church here. We started going there when we moved here, then decided to just go here on a regular basis. We thought why spend all that gas to go all that way when there are good churches here in town. Wouldn't you agree? I don't know what I can help you with about the church at Dutch Mills."

"We are asking a few questions, that's all."

"Sure," she said.

"You have heard about the situation there, haven't you?" Colton asked. A friend of this woman, Kelli, the church organist, had already told them she called Karen that Friday evening, telling her all she knew at the time.

"Of course. I have a good friend at Dutch Mills who called and told me all about it.

In fact, she said she was the one who found Maureen's body, so, naturally, she was pretty shook up about it."

So far, so good, Colton thought.

Most people did not have a reason to deviate from the truth, but it was always a good sign when everything jelled from the get-go.

Karen was continuing, "I can't imagine finding a person like that and Kelli said the intruder had shot the dog, also. What was it, a burglary gone wrong?"

"Well, we don't know anything yet. We are still investigating."

Colton could imagine what she was thinking. This was two months after the murder and there still had not been an arrest, or even any suspects, for that matter.

Her and everyone else, Colton thought. *People are really getting antsy.*

"Do you own a vehicle, ma'am?" Colton asked.

She looked surprised at the question, as most people had when he had asked.

"Well…yes…of course. What does that have to do with anything?" She asked that with more surprise than anything. Same question everyone asked, more out of surprise than anything else.

"Do you mind if we have a look at it? We have a warrant."

Eric held it up. He had to hand it to her when she reached out for it.

She read it all. It looked legitimate and the signature above the seal was in blue ink, which was legal.

"Just a minute," she said. "I have to go back through the house to open the garage door."

Before they had time to say anything else, she unlocked the front door and just as quickly shut it behind her. In a few seconds they heard the garage door start up. By the time it had gone all the way, she was at the back of her car.

"Why are you searching and vacuuming cars?" she asked. That was what the warrant permitted, a search and thorough vacuuming of the vehicle.

"Dog hairs," came the answer.

"Dog hairs?" she asked, incredulously.

"Was the dog killed in a car, and you're trying to locate it? The car, I mean," she asked.

"Well, no, it wasn't, but we are hoping to find any dog hairs, or even one hair, that might match that of the dog."

"How could that happen?" she asked. She had a puzzled look on her face.

Colton figured that she was trying to picture that scenario.

"Just an angle of the investigation that we are following. Do you mind?"

As they were talking Eric had gone to the patrol car. He was back with a hand-held

car vac.

"Be my guest," she said, as she stepped aside. She pushed a button on the fob and the doors of the car opened. Another push made the trunk open.

She stood and watched as they searched and vacuumed the car. She knew they would not find anything and wondered about this tack.

They really must not have any clues at all, she thought. *This is really grasping at straws, I would think.*

"Do you have a dog?" Colton asked. He had seen several hairs on the mat on the front floorboard.

"No, I don't, but you might find some dog hairs in there. I keep a lint brush here in the garage to use before I go into the house. I'm sure my cat smells dog scent on my pants, anyway."

"How so the hairs?" he asked.

"I go down to Dutch Mills every six weeks to have my hair cut by a friend there. Not the one you talked to, but another one. They live three miles south, on past Dutch Mills. I haven't turned into Dutch Mills, itself, for longer than I can remember. I am going down there tomorrow, in fact. Not into Dutch Mills, itself, but on south to have my hair cut."

She touched her hair. "Tomorrow is my regular appointment day and I am getting a little shaggy, don't you think?"

"The hairs?"

"Oh, yeah. My friends have two dogs, two outside dogs. They know me, of course, the dogs I mean, and one always jumps on me, both coming and going. He is a large, shaggy dog and he really sheds. I never insult my friends by standing by my car and brushing myself before I get in when I'm leaving. When I go down, I spend the day. My friend cuts my hair about 10:00 in the morning, we have lunch, then we, that's my friend, her husband, who is also a friend, of course, and I, play cards or games all afternoon.

"I'm always home by dark, though. I just don't like to drive at night, the lights of the oncoming traffic seem to all go together.

"So, you will probably find hairs from those two dogs in my car. I have to admit I did not vacuum it since my last trip there."

Why did I think at first that this woman was a quiet person? No wonder she is friends with the organist. They both talk, well, ramble really, at about ninety words a minute.

Colton was tired. He was sure this was a dead end. He was sure the dog hairs from this car would match those of her friend's dogs, but, again, he was leaving no stone unturned. When asked at any time, he wanted to be able to say they were investigating any angle they could think of in connection with this case.

The Devil was in the details.

They thanked her for her cooperation. As they drove away, she walked back through the garage to the side door to the house, where she pushed the button to lower the garage door.

Dogs! What an insult!

Chapter 25

This short stretch of South Arkansas Highway 244 was only about two miles long. They were at this point in their trips to various homeowners in their designated area around Dutch Mills, the hair-brained investigation still ongoing.

There were only three houses on this short stretch before the highway became Oklahoma Highway 51. They planned to interview the two today that they had not had the opportunity or time to do so the other trip down here.

The first house, on the right, proved to be that of the resident, large farmer of the area. He owned most of the open pasture land between Highway 59 and the Oklahoma line. The only thing preventing him from owning all the land here was the next home down, which resided on a small acreage.

After interviewing this couple and vacuuming all three vehicles, a car, a large dual-axle pickup (which obviously pulled the large cattle hauler they saw in the barnyard), and another, older pickup which the man explained was only used here on the farm, to take bales of hay or salt licks, or whatever to the cattle across the fields.

Naturally, they were both at home the night of the murder.

And just as naturally, both Colton and Eric knew the three bags containing the vacuumed contents of the vehicles, would probably not yield the matching dog hair, although the wife had admitted she took one of their own dogs to the vet a couple of weeks before.

Almost everyone had a dog, of one sort or another, in this part of the country. Most were outside dogs, meant to be guard dogs if anyone came onto the property. They probably did a very effective job.

The next driveway on the right was at an angle, going to a small house. There were two vehicles in the driveway, a burgundy Dodge Ram and a dark blue Ford Taurus. Neither was new. Both vehicles badly needed a wash and you could barely see the license plates. Either certainly not the smallish white car reported by Henry Carlton.

Only by Henry Carlton. Ricky had not been able to identify the car.

Colton couldn't forget that. This whole ordeal might turn into a "he said/she said" situation.

A man came out of the storage shed on the right when he heard the sheriff's vehicle coming up the driveway. He was wiping his hands on a dirty rag. He must have been working on something.

As Colton and Eric got out, he said, "Howdy, officers. What can I do you for?"

He laughed at his own wit.

"I am Washington County Sheriff Colton Mitchell and this is my Chief Deputy, Eric Simmons. We would like to ask you a few questions concerning an ongoing investigation with our department. Are you the only one home right now?"

"No, my wife's here. Just a minute."

The man climbed the front steps and yelled, "Honey, come here. There are two county officers that want to talk to us."

The front door immediately opened, and a middle-aged woman came out, all smiles.

"Hi, officers, how are you?" she asked. "Would you like some iced tea? Would you like to come inside and sit down?"

"Oh, no, that's not necessary, to either, but thank you."

If the inside of the home looked anything like the outside, they didn't want to go in.

"Part of our investigation will involve your vehicles, anyway, so we need to just stay outside."

"Well, I'm glad it's a nice day," she said.

"Does this involve the murder of the pastor's wife at Dutch Mills?" the man asked.

"That's such a terrible thing. Who would do such a thing? Robbery gone wrong, most people are saying. I heard you guys were going around asking questions and vacuuming vehicles. Really, are you vacuuming vehicles? Ours could sure use it!"

He laughed again and his wife joined in.

Colton and Eric smiled. They did not want to antagonize anyone.

They asked the usual questions of where were they that night and next morning.

"Well, I was here, but there's no one to verify that but myself. My wife, here, was visiting her sister in Siloam."

They turned their attention to the wife.

"Would you tell us about that?" Colton asked.

Anybody out of their usual place, their own homes and beds, that evening and early morning, was questioned just a little more than usual.

"It was a planned trip. I had not stayed, or even visited, with my sister for a long time. When she called and suggested I stay a few nights that weekend with her, why not just come to her house after work that Thursday and stay that night and Friday night, I thought why not? Wayne here," she gestured toward her husband, "never minds when I go visit someone, especially not my sister. So, there I went. She can verify all this."

"I'm sure she can. If you will give us her name and address, we will have to check, you understand."

"Of course," she agreed, "just let me run in and write that down for you."

Before they could ask her wait, she was gone.

In the meantime, they gave the warrant to Wayne and started cleaning and vacuuming the vehicles. It was going to take a while. Like the yard, there were items everywhere in the vehicles.

Wonder what they do if they have passengers? Eric thought. *There's nowhere to put your feet for all the trash, empty soda containers, complete with lids and straws, candy wrappers, and no telling what else!*

The wife returned with the name and address. Colton tucked the paper in his front pocket. She asked what they were looking for. When they mentioned dog hairs, she exclaimed, "Oh, wait!"

She ran back inside the house and returned with a small dog. Colton straightened from vacuuming the pickup to look at the dog.

"Isn't this just the cutest little thing you have ever seen?" she asked. She was beaming. Quite obviously, she thought so.

Colton had to admit he was looking at the cutest mutt he had ever seen, and told her how cute it was.

"You'll find his hairs in the Taurus, I'm afraid. We had to take him to the vet a few days ago. He just had a cold, though, so you have nothing to worry about. He was moping around, not himself at all, so we feared the worst, of course."

She looked down at the dog. "But you're fine, aren't you, you handsome thing?"

All this was in baby talk, to the dog, as people tend to do to their pets, especially the small, cute ones.

The wife talked nonstop, which made Colton wonder again if everyone in Dutch Mills had taken a college course in How to Chatter Nonstop 101, or maybe it was even a graduate course. Whichever, the residents around here tended to either clam up or talk forever, sometimes wondering off subject, as this woman was about to do. Colton could feel it. She was saying something about the dog being dropped on them, since they lived out here in the country, and all that, and was starting a discourse on why people always do that.

He cut her short. Fortunately, they were finished vacuuming the vehicles and said they really needed to go, thank you for your time.

Chapter 26

Next, they drove just kitty-corned across the high-way and went down a gravel road that the couple they just spoke to referred to as "Chalk Bluff Road," which was not the name on the sign. Another one of those re-named for 911 purposes. They said if you took the first turn on the right, the road took you back into Oklahoma, you were just not aware when you entered Oklahoma from that road.

That put about a half dozen houses down this road and the one toward the west going into Oklahoma.

They had time for just this one more.

They turned around opposite this white house. It was an old house but looked interesting. It was built in the style before the turn of the century. That was the twentieth century, of course.

Two dogs, one a very large, black one and another smaller one came to the front fence, barking at the two strangers. That brought the woman of the house to the front door.

She called to the dogs and told them to go around back, which they did, to the surprise of the two men.

She came to the gate and let them in. They explained why they were there.

All of a sudden it dawned on Colton that this must be the woman that cut the hair of the woman they talked with in Siloam Springs.

It was. They were friends. She verified that there might be dog hairs in her friend's car. The two dogs always welcomed her by jumping up on her when she came.

Yes, they were both here and asleep, getting up at their usual time on the night and morning of the murder, wasn't that an awful thing?

The man had come out to the front yard. They agreed that they now locked their doors, when before they thought the dogs in the yard were enough, but since the other dog had been shot, it didn't seem to be quite enough protection. It was hard to think there might be a murderer living in Dutch Mills, or around in the countryside somewhere.

When Colton commented on the house, they beamed. They had put a lot of money in remodeling the house, putting in an extra bathroom and all, but it had originally been a watering stop for the old Butterfield Stagecoach Mail route, a line that went from Missouri down to Fort Smith, about thirty miles south.

A previous owner, who was now deceased, had owned the house from 1968 – 1978 before moving across the highway. She had wanted to make a driveway coming off Highway 244 and provide pie and coffee to travelers from Dutch Mills and the Arkansas side who went to shop or visit in Stilwell, Oklahoma, some seven miles to the west.

At the time, the back bedroom was a well, with a covering, but still functioning as a hand-drawn well with water in it. This was where the horses were watered during the mail route days, as well as the passengers. There were no overnight faculties for passengers, but a space for a well-deserved rest.

She wanted to search and find memorabilia from the Butterfield Stagecoach and put it on the walls and share the history of the house with visitors.

She never built the rest stop, though. The husband was never in favor of it, so there went one dream, as dreams have a way of going out of our lives. But she always talked of it, even after she moved across the highway. She had been a friend of this couple.

At one time, you could walk south down Chalk Bluff Road and see the cleared space of the trail, between trees. It was right beside the road. Unfortunately, a person who bought the dairy at the end of the road, graded the ditch on the east side and all but obliterated the trail. If you did not know it had been there before, now there was no evidence. Evidently, this new person had not been told of the historical significance of this part of the trail.

The Butterfield Overland Mail Trail Route had been a major factor in the settlement and development of Arkansas. Settlements sprang up all along the mail route. People were always eager to get mail from the outside world.

There were currently many sites from the Missouri line to Fort Smith, including some in Fayetteville, commemorating this trail, but this section had been forgotten, probably because no one could now find the trail.

This current owner knew her friend that lived in Siloam also could recognize where the trail began about five miles north of Dutch Mills, where Highway 59 curved. For years and years, there was a clearing through the forest that went straight ahead, then connected to the paved highway several miles south.

That was the clearing of the Butterfield route. But it was rapidly being overtaken by trees and brush. Unfortunately, now, only the older folk around would know, if they even were told about it. If some of these older residents in the area did not contact someone in a historical society, it would forever be lost.

Eric was a history buff, so he found this fascinating. He knew about the Butterfield Mail Trail, but not this little particular part.

They showed him where the well was located, now under the floor of a master bedroom. The fireplace in the living room was the original brick. They even had the original andirons in the fireplace. They had come with the house when it was sold. This original fireplace still worked.

Man, Eric thought, *they sure don't make things like they used to. To have this fireplace still here, still working. It is amazing, really, and the history has been lost to most of the people around here.*

Colton and Eric spent more time at this place than they had at any place previously, but it was because of Eric's interest in the history.

After vacuuming the vehicles, a pickup and a car, Colton and Eric left. This would be their last visit on this case for the day.

They were not too hopeful of these two bags, either.

Chapter 27

Kelli called Karen in the middle of the afternoon one Sunday.

"Guess what? We all knew it was going to happen, sooner or later, and it has happened. I can't blame him, really, I would have been gone before now."

Karen knew her friend. This could be about anything.

"What are you talking about? And who doesn't you blame for what?"

"It's Pastor Jennings. There are rumors that he is talking about moving, that he can't stand to stay in Dutch Mills any longer. I just knew that was coming, didn't you? After all, why should he stay? Everyone is still looking at everyone else as a possible killer. It seems every time Pastor Jennings walks into a room, people are surprised he's still here." Kelli took a deep breath and Karen was thankful. Her friend did this, but usually Karen was able to get a few words in here and there.

"I really can't blame him for wanting to leave, can you? I don't think I would want to stay in the same community, living alone, where my spouse had been murdered. Besides, what if the killer decided to come back and finish the job? Maybe he was really after both of them, has anyone thought of that?"

Karen was able to get those few words in.

There was a hesitation on the line.

"No, well, no," Kelli said, tentatively. "Nothing has been said about that. Maybe no one has thought of that. Do you really think so?"

"I have no idea, of course, it was just something I threw out there to agree with him about not staying in the same house where his wife was murdered."

"Of course, if the killer is watching, he would know that the pastor is staying in the old parsonage, wouldn't he? If he wanted to kill the pastor, also, couldn't he kill him from there?"

Kelli was clearly agitated with this thought.

Karen groaned inwardly.

Now, why did I say that so offhand like that? I should know things like that always plant a bug in Kelli's ear, so she runs with it. I could kick myself, Karen thought.

"Just forget I said that, okay?" she said to her friend. "I was just being silly. So, calm down, okay? You said you stopped going to your therapist now that Maureen is gone, so don't get worked up about something that is really nothing to the point you have to go back. You are making such great strides."

"Yes, I am, aren't I?" Kelli agreed.

They chatted for a few more minutes, long enough for Karen to feel Kelli was calm again.

Then, they hung up.

Chapter 28

The men encountered a forced hiatus from their interviews with the case because there was a scheduled conference of all the country sheriffs in the State of Arkansas. Also invited this year were their chief deputies. This year they had deviated from the norm of a summer conference to one in late September.

This year the conference was in Fayetteville because the city had completed construction on new convention facilities with the capability of handling this many, plus speakers, and lodging for all guests. New and larger lodging families in the area could accommodate outside guests. This was all due to the growth of Northwest Arkansas.

Both men were not opposed to taking a break, although there was always mounting pressure from the public and county officials to identify and arrest someone for the murder. The general public just did not understand that if there was no evidence and no clues, how could they arrest anyone? But the pressure was always there, even if not spoken.

People needed a scapegoat. The whole department was playing it pretty close to the chest, though, and nothing was revealed, especially not Colton's "hair-brained" scheme. Surely someone would scream about a waste of time and monetary resources.

Colton just still had his feelings about it.

This evening, Wednesday evening, Clark, Colton's former chief deputy and now Marion County Sheriff, and his wife were visiting at Colton's home.

True to the invitation, they were staying with the Mitchell during this conference so they could catch up on personal and business news. The two women were great friends, so there was that.

Right now, the two men were sitting on the patio, sipping beer, waiting for the charcoal to die down in the grill so they could put the steaks on.

"You realize that whatever money I might be saving by not staying in a hotel and eating out every meal, Nancy is going to make up for at Macy's, or wherever. I know the ladies are planning a major shopping trip tomorrow," Clark said.

"I know, I know," Colton replied. "I saw in the paper that Macy's is having a great sale. The word "sale" seems to be irresistible to Marsha, especially Macy's. She loves that store. When she learned there was one here in the mall in Fayetteville, she knew she wanted to move here!"

Colton laughed. "I tease her about it, it wasn't the only reason to move here, of course, it just didn't hurt!"

"I know what you're saying," Clark responded, also laughing.

The couple had arrived that day in plenty of time to come to the house, settle their suitcases in the guest room, then the men went to the opening meetings of the conference.

This first day had been the business end of the conference. Various officers of the association were presented and voted on, other representatives of different committees, that sort of thing.

Tomorrow would be a main part of the conference, with the keynote speaker being the Adair County, Oklahoma sheriff, Quinton Adair. Colton knew for sure the name of the county had a lot to do with the election of a man with the same last name.

But this man had proved to be willing to work for his people. The Adair County Sheriff's Department had implemented a major drug elimination program and had been quite successful. The main emphasis had been on the searching out and eliminating marijuana fields by the use of infra-red cameras and equipment.

Low-flying, stealth aircraft flew over the area, pinpointing the plants. Raids were then conducted, men and women arrested, and the field torched, after bagging some as evidence.

Colton and Clark discussed how difficult it must have been to not have arrested friends and relatives. One or two had to be arrested, of course, to make the program look fair to all. Sheriff Adair remained popular, in spite of the arrests of relatives.

So, he was presenting the "nuts and bolts" of the program to the Arkansas sheriffs and how they carried it out to the success it had been in Adair County. With Washington County bordering on Adair County, Colton had already engaged the aid of Quinton in the current case.

Places like the south end of Dutch Mills South (excuse me, State Line Road), ended within a few feet of the Oklahoma line. Colton explained this to Clark. At the last mailbox on that road, if you took two steps behind the mailbox, you were in Oklahoma.

"Wow!" Clark said. "Here's a question for you. What if you happened upon a body that had been thrown from a vehicle, or even killed right there on that spot, and half the body was in Oklahoma and the other half in Arkansas, whose jurisdiction would it be in, yours or Quinton's? What would you do?"

Colton laughed.

"After this case, or in the middle of it, like we are? I think I would put on a pair of disposable gloves and gently roll the body over to the Oklahoma side. Then, I would leave and let someone else discover the body. Or, would it be FBI since it would be state-to-state?"

Now it was Clark's turn to laugh.

"You would not," Clark responded. "If I know you, you wouldn't do that. But it makes for an interesting scenario doesn't it? I don't think I would like to be bordering on another state like that. Too much confusion. I look forward to hearing Quinton, though, and what happened. It's not finished, from what I heard."

"It's actually an ongoing program with them."

The charcoal was going to be ready in a few more minutes to put the steaks on. The wives were still in the kitchen, chopping the veggies for the salad and preparing other items.

At first, they thought Abby might be able to join them, but a test was announced in one of her classes for this Friday, so she thought she would just stay in her room and study.

She was a month into her sophomore year and was eligible for living off campus, or, as she had chosen, to live in the sorority house.

Colton and Marsha had briefly panicked at first, recalling all the horror stories they had heard about sororities and fraternities and the "Greek" life at this point of time. Perhaps they even remembered some of their young, less settled days, compared to now, of course. But had it really changed that much?

Abby reassured them that she had a good head on her shoulders, knew what she was striving for, and that was that. So far, she had not indulged in any of the keggers or frat parties. Although she was well-liked and enjoyed the popularity she had gained as a cheerleader, she had stayed away from those stories and rumors, also. Not all cheerleaders were "friends" with all the athletes. She'd made certain decisions from the first day she set foot on the campus and had stuck by those decisions.

Clark and Nancy were sorry to miss her, since they had known her all her life, but they understood. Maybe next time.

They had not talked about this current case of Colton's, and they knew they needed to. At least Colton needed to.

"No leads on the killer?" Clark asked. He did not even have to say what case he was talking about. Colton knew.

"No, but let me tell you about the most likely suspect. Maybe, though, he is that only because he looks and acts the part. I can't tell."

"Well, if you can't tell, I don't know who could," Clark responded. "You've always had such good instincts about people."

Colton told him about the questioning of Henry Carlton, who lead them to his son, Ricky, and their accounts of the night.

"You see, I have the dad, Mr. Carlton, who is the only one who saw the small, whitish car. Ricky couldn't say what he saw. Carlton's wife wasn't even out of bed yet to go on their trip. Then there is Ricky, the son. Then, these three vehicles could have collided in the heavy storm. They must have been within seconds and inches of each other.

"The son admitted that he met a vehicle on Cane Hill Road, sorry Highway 45, but couldn't tell anything about it, whether pickup, SUV, or car, because of the storm. Then, when he got to the end of 45, to go left (you can't go straight), he decided to sit there and wait for a few minutes for the storm to let up, since he wasn't feeling his best.

"And I don't doubt that, if he told the truth about the amount of beer and alcohol he must have consumed at The Oasis," Colton interjected his own thought here.

"According to him, he put on his emergency flashers and was glad he did. A minute after he stopped, a car emerged out of the rain going north on Highway 59 and went straight. He said that, if he had made the turn left when he thought to, that car would have most likely have hit him. Visibility was so bad he sat there for a good ten minutes before he slowly turned onto 59, then crept along at about 15 miles per hour to Dutch Mills and his folks' house. There he saw another car.

"He said he got there somewhere around 4:00 a.m. It took him that long from The Oasis in the storm, according to him.

"This makes the father or the son or the father and the son, together, our most likely suspects for the murder. They were right at the bottom of the hill from the house at the same time, or close enough for government work, as they say, to have killed her."

"The timing, for both, or all three vehicles, is certainly a strange coincidence, but I do see it as a coincidence, only. You really do have the he said/she said predicament here. Anything else?" Clark asked.

"I must be tired," Colton admitted. "The next neighbor down from the Carltons, to the south, did not hear Ricky's pickup come home, but when he went to milk the Carltons' cow about 6 a.m., he saw it. As he was milking, he heard it start up and drive away. Henry Carlton never saw his son come. He might have been the vehicle that met Ricky on Highway 45, since they were headed east and didn't recognize him in the storm, either. We don't know that for sure."

"Yeah, very strange and unusual, but still circumstantial," Clark pointed out.

"Hey, here comes Marsha with the steaks. Let's get them on. I'm starving right now. I'm glad it doesn't take long on the grill. Let's finish this later, okay?"

The steaks were perfect, as was the rest of the meal.

They continued the conversation about the case while the wives cleaned. They offered to do the dishes, but Marsha insisted they talk and catch up on everything.

"We still have some more homeowners to interview and vacuum their vehicles."

Clark almost choked on his beer when Colton said that.

"How is that going, anyway? Has that worked as a kind of strategy for catching a killer?"

"Just one of those feelings you get sometimes. Just a 'feel it in your cells' type of thing and I went with it. At least it keeps the men busy and working toward a goal. It is certainly keeping the forensics techs in the lab busy, going through the bags speck of dust by speck of dust.

Clark laughed.

"It certainly does seem pretty far-fetched, even the first time you told me you were going to do it. I thought you were probably kidding, but I see that you're serious."

"Dead serious," Colton said, then groaned. "Sorry, bad choice of expression, in this case."

"Good luck with that," Clark responded. He meant it.

Colton just may know what he is doing, he thought. Stranger things had happened.

Chapter 29

Somehow, when the phone rang, Karen knew it was going to be Kelli. Who else called her this early in the morning?

It was.

"Guess what?" Kelli began, when Karen had said "Hello?"

"What?" she asked. But she knew this was probably going to be something about the murder of Maureen. Kelli had called her many times over the past several months about this case, speculating first one thing and another, telling her what this person said and that person said, what she overheard at church, just everything she could think of. Maybe some things she just made up.

Karen had no way of knowing. This was really the only person she talked to from Dutch Mills, aside from the friend that cut her hair every six weeks. Oh, maybe they talked in between that time, to verify the appointment, what to eat, and things like that. Their main talking time for catching up on things was when Karen went down for the appointment and spent the day there.

And there was her sister, but their talks were very infrequent. They never had really talked to each other much, not even before their mother had passed away.

Diane had moved into the mother's place. She had even sold all the mother's possessions at an auction without telling Karen she was going to, so that was "still in the air." Karen did not want to go through the things in the dead of winter, when their mother had passed away, so she just assumed—but you know what they say about that—that the sister would wait until a nice, spring day and Karen would come and go through things, keeping what she wanted.

One of Karen's sons had even said he wanted to see what he wanted of his grandma's things, to have to remember her by, so there was that.

At least in the first few days after their mother's death, Karen had quickly taken some quilts her mother had made by hand and a few other items. After all, she was the oldest, she had a right to keep what she wanted.

So, this call really had to be from Kelli. Diane was already at work at the University of Arkansas at Fayetteville.

"Are you going to tell me 'what' or not?" Karen asked.

"This morning, during morning worship service, Pastor Jennings announced that he was leaving. He's returning home to Florida. He said he didn't know if he was going to take another church yet, or not, that he hadn't been looking, but he felt he could no longer stay at our church.

"You know, of course, that he couldn't stay in the parsonage after what had happened. Since the old parsonage was still empty, the real estate lady convinced the owner and he agreed a couple of months ago to let Pastor Jennings live there. He took a bedroom suite out of the parsonage, out of one of the guest bedrooms, since, of course, he couldn't stand to be in the same bed where Maureen had been killed, you can understand that, of course, and he took the sofa, a couple of chairs, and the dining suite, just enough to enable him to live in the old parsonage. Luckily, all the kitchen appliances were in the old house, part of the package to help sell it, I guess. Oh, yeah, he took the microwave, coffee pot, things like that out of the kitchen that he needed to live there.

"But, after a while, he just couldn't be here, in Dutch Mills, any longer. You can understand that, can't you?"

"Of course," Karen answered. "I'm surprised he stayed this long. I always had the impression that the little church there was just a stepping stone on their way to bigger and better things. After all, they went to seminary on the West Coast, so this position got them halfway to Florida, so why not take it? At least, that has always been my opinion."

Kelli continued with her own thoughts, as if Karen had not entered the conversation at all.

"I'm glad you haven't been at church here the last few months. Well, I don't mean it that way, you know what I mean. I would have enjoyed having you at church, it's just that the feeling in the air has been incredible. You can cut the tension with a knife, as the expression goes. We have been down to around fifty people, just fifty people, for the last two months. Only those from the old families that have always gone here have been the ones coming.

"If anyone else comes, it seems they are always looking around, wondering if the person here or there is the killer, and if they are next.

"Personally, I still think it was a robbery gone wrong, possibly someone just traveling down Highway 59, and the person, or persons, are long gone now. I can't imagine it being anyone from the church.

"And I don't know how the church is going to keep up with the payments for that new addition those people voted to have built. With only fifty people coming, maybe even less of them giving, what's going to happen there? You know I voted against the new addition, saying the church didn't have the money, what if something came up and we couldn't afford the loan payments. And, now, look what *did* come up! I can't blame people for not wanting to come now."

She paused, which again allowed Karen to get a comment in the conversation.

"What you mean is, you don't want to think that it might be anyone from the church or the community. Kelli," Karen began, seriously, ignoring the part about the money, "you know that you are not the only one she didn't get along with, if we can put it mildly, not within the church or in the community. Those people around there hold grudges. You forget that I've been around there for many years. I've known a lot of those people for many decades now. I know what they are like. They either like you and accept you or they don't. It's that simple. Just one 'run-in' with Maureen would have been enough for one person to resent it forever and decide to do something about it. You know all this as well as I do. You may have moved away as an adult, but your mom would have told things over the years."

Kelli drew in her breath.

"Do you have someone in mind? Someone you think did it?"

Karen laughed.

"Of course not," she responded. "I've been away from there for a couple of years. I know the people over the years, the older ones, but I have no idea who has been coming there for these two years. That was just a thought I had, but it's as good a thought as any, don't you agree?"

Karen realized she should not have said all she did. It just gave Kelli something else to worry about, but it was too late to take it back.

"But don't worry about what I just said, I was just blowing steam. You know it's best for the pastor to go home and try to make a new life the best he can. Since he and Maureen never had children, I'm sure he'll now meet and marry someone else and have a house full of children running around everywhere."

She was doing her best, now, to get Kelli's mind back on the pastor and away from any comments she made earlier. No use adding to Kelli's stress. She had really started to calm down these last two months, away from Maureen, and even was better than from the last time they had talked.

"I still just hope no one thinks I had anything to do with it," Kelli said.

"Oh, I'm sure they don't," Karen said, in a calming voice. "As I said, you weren't the only one who disliked Maureen."

"Yeah, you're right." Kelli sighed.

"Thanks for listening," she said. "You always make me feel better when I call to talk with you. And I seem to need to pretty often, don't I?"

Kelli laughed.

"That's all right. What are friends for, anyway?"

In a few more minutes, they hung up. Karen knew it wouldn't be the last call. But she meant what she said to Kelli.

What *were* friends for?

Chapter 30

Several months had gone by and the Sheriff's Department was being pressured to find the "Dutch Mills Killer." The assigned teams had faithfully conducted interviews and vacuumed vehicles. The lab techs had just as faithfully examined every particle of dust and whatever was in the bags.

Nothing that could be used as evidence.

At least no dog hairs belong to the pastor's dog.

This Friday, late afternoon, at the end of the work week for most of the staff, there were only the usual three left in the building.

The usual three plus two, that is.

Colton asked Eric to stay a few minutes after 5:00. Eric took a seat across from Colton at his desk.

"All things considered, the only possible, logical suspect we have in the Dutch Mills case is Ricky Carlton. Wouldn't you agree?"

Colton looked at his deputy. They had discussed this off and on without coming to any conclusion. Usually, they would be interrupted. Colton hoped this would be the last discussion. He had asked not to be disturbed, no calls, not even Marsha. This was just too important right now.

Eric shrugged. "He has always seemed the logical suspect, in my mind. This thing about the dog hairs…"

He didn't complete his thought. He looked at Colton.

"Oh, don't worry, you won't offend me. I know what the men call my theory about the dog hairs, have always known from the beginning. I don't know who started calling it "The Hair-brained Theory," but he or she just might prove to be correct. Let's look at the complete facts of this case as they apply to Ricky."

He straightened up in his chair. He pulled a notepad toward him and reached for a pen. He pushed a duplicate pad and pen toward Eric so he could write down the same thing. If one or the other thought of something they both didn't together, it could be added.

Funny, the use of the notebook. It seemed to be the thing Colton always did during an investigation. As high-tech as a computer or phone might be, he still found himself writing his thoughts out long-hand, on paper.

"First thing," Colton began. "we have Henry Carlton's account of seeing a 'small, whitish' car parked down at the end of his property around 3:50 or 4:00 a.m. that Friday morning. He was up and stepped out on his porch because he couldn't sleep before their planned trip to the wife's sister. We only have his word and the son about this vehicle. No one else saw it and Carlton himself did not get a perfect look at it because of the heavy rain that was falling and thick bushes in the way. What's next? I can't seem to put it together all of a sudden. I guess I've thought of it too much."

Colton stood up. He went to the small, personal coffee stand that was in his office.

"Coffee?" he asked Eric. He held up the coffee pot toward him. "It's fairly fresh, made just before you came in."

"Yeah, I spelled the aroma of your favorite blend, which I do like, you know, but I don't think I'll have any just now."

Colton poured his coffee and returned to his desk.

"Now, where were we?" he asked.

"What happened after Carlton saw the vehicle."

"Oh, yeah. He couldn't tell if the car left or not, thought he saw lights flickering through the trees going south on Highway 59, but who knew if it was that same vehicle. Then, they left on their trip. They took Highway 45 through Cane Hill to connect to Highway 62 just east of Lincoln where they meet and turned right (you can't go straight). He said that just as he turned onto Highway 45, a vehicle was parked well off the other side at the intersection. He figured it was riding out the storm before continuing. But, because he was turning and didn't see the vehicle in the rain until he was right upon it, he was too involved in missing the vehicle that he didn't pay too much attention to what it was, except it was a pickup.

"Ricky said he met a vehicle in about that same spot, but said the same thing as his dad. He couldn't tell what type of vehicle it was, just the pickup part as they passed. But the time frame is right for what they both said.

"Ricky reaches the Highway45 turnoff where it meets Highway 59 and before he can turn south (you can't go straight), a vehicle comes out of the storm going north. Now, this may or may not have been the same vehicle, having turned around to come north. Why would it have gone south on Highway 59 if that was not the way it needed to go to go home or wherever."

Colton stopped to take a breath.

Eric continued.

"We've talked about coincidences and the fact that we just don't believe in them. We've both seen too much in this line of work to what everything happens, or happened, for a reason. Personally, if it is only a coincidence that all three of these vehicles were practically in the same spot at the same time, which was the perfect time for the murder, then it would be the strangest thing I have ever heard of. That goes wa-a-y beyond Murphy's Law."

Colton assumed he was referring to the old epigram "anything that can go wrong, will go wrong," and a lot of people have added "at the worst possible moment," which would apply in this case.

The perfect storm, so to speak.

Eric continued. "Ricky confessed that he really didn't remember, completely, making it to Dutch Mills and getting to his dad's house, going into the house and crashing in the small back bedroom. Almost hitting a car at the corner because there never is one parked there. We're sure he was drunk, that was the reason it took him so long to get from The Oasis to Dutch Mills. It took him almost twice the time as normal. But there was the storm, also."

Eric shrugged. "I know I've pulled off the road at times to wait a while during some of these thunderstorms around here. It's almost typical weather here, just that some are worse than others."

Colton continued. "Ricky admits that he doesn't remember anything about that time. I'm sure he just made it to the house and bed because it was such a familiar thing for him to do. Why couldn't he have gone up the hill to the right, up to the parsonage, instead of turning left for the short distance to the Carlton house? What if he then realized where he was and thought this was the perfect opportunity to 'take care of,' or 'get back at,' this woman he didn't like, who wouldn't leave him alone, because all evidence would be covered by the storm. He probably thought they were both home, but you know how drunk people are, he could have thought he could handle both of them, especially surprising them in the middle of the night. An added bonus was when there was only the woman at home."

"And the gun?" Colton asked.

"Well, when we talked to him, he wasn't going to confess to having such a weapon. The age of it says it could have belonged to Mr. Carlton and Ricky came in possession of it somewhere along the years. Mr. Carlton may not even know it is missing, probably thinks it's tucked away in the back of his closet or back of a little-used drawer, behind the extra linens or something. He seemed the type that might snitch the gun when the parents weren't looking."

"That's certainly a possibility. I hadn't thought of all this before," Colton grinned. "That's why you're my chief deputy and that's why I asked you to stay right now. Even after all I can think of in any situation, you seem to think of more, and better. Let's certainly put that down as a possibility."

There was a pause in the conversation as each of the men wrote in their notebooks.

"I can't say that's really the case, or I would be sheriff and not you, but I can come up with some strange ideas, sometimes, I do admit."

"They certainly aren't all that strange, but you realize that everything we have is all circumstantial."

"There's another question I just thought of," Eric said. "Why was it so important to the Carltons that they leave for their trip in the middle of such a terrible storm like that? Don't you think they could have waited a little while longer until the rain lessened? They are both retired, as well as the sister and her husband, so why the rush?"

"Good point," Colton returned. "See how smart you are. Let's put that all together in a few minutes."

"I do realize that," Eric said, grinning. He referred to the smart part. "But let's make that list, anyway," he concluded.

They both worked silently for the next several minutes, compared notes, then came up with a list of events, according to the timeline:

1.   According to coroner, death occurred around 4:00 to 4:30 a.m.

2.   At around 3:50 a.m., Henry Carlton sees what he describes as a "small, whitish" car at the end of his property, just at the junction of the roads to go either up the hill to the parsonage, or straight (but only a few houses down this way, north, in the community, then the road ends at the creek), or turn toward Highway 59.

3.   Carlton doesn't see the headlights go on and sees flickering through the trees on 59 South, but he loses the lights intermittently in the heavy rain and trees. He assumes the vehicle turned north (you can't go straight), which he could not see because there is a house in the line of sight. He said/she said on both #2 and #3. Carlton and son were the only ones to see this vehicle.

4.   They leave to go on their trip, when they turn onto Highway 45, a vehicle is parked there, they nearly hit it, not expecting a vehicle there at this time of the morning, but he recalls nothing but that it is a pickup, probably riding out the storm.

5.   The pickup belongs to Ricky Carlton, who said he did ride out the storm there at the intersection for a few minutes. As he was parked there, a vehicle came out of the storm going north on Highway 59. He couldn't tell what the vehicle was in the heavy rain.

6.   In a few minutes, out of nowhere, it seemed, there came another vehicle that turned onto Highway 59, almost hitting him, although he had on his flashing hazard lights. He thought it was a pickup, but went by so quickly (and probably he was too drunk) to get a good look at it.

7.   According to Ricky, in a few minutes, when the rain let up, he continued to Dutch Mills, the Carlton house, went in the back door and crashed in the small bedroom. He nearly hit a car at the corner.

8.   Ricky woke up early and decided since no one was home, probably one of the trips to his aunt that he might as well go on home, check on Ralph.

9.   No dog hairs matching the dog from the crime scene in either Henry or Ricky's pickups. Dead end there.

10. No other logical suspects.

11. No dog hairs in any vehicle.

They both leaned back in their chairs.

"We have enough circumstantial evidence, simply because of these perfect timings,

to think that Ricky had plenty of time and opportunity to commit the crime. He had motive, the confrontations he had over a year or so with the pastor's wife. Some people, we would have to agree, just can't let things like that go, and drunks can really start building things in their minds to something they really aren't. We get those situations all the time."

Colton was thinking out loud with all this.

"Yeah, the old 'mountain out of a molehill' thing," Eric agreed. "I have another thought. You're forgetting that the forensic lab techs, after their weekly report today, still have about a half dozen evidence bags to go through from vehicles. We aren't through with that angle yet, your 'hair-brained' theory. And I've even thought of something else."

Colton looked up.

"What if the father and son were in on it together? What if they had it planned for the next severe storm that came through, and it just happened that the pastor was out of town? Parents can be pretty protective of their children, even if they don't always agree with what they are doing, even bad-mouth them sometimes. Or, what if the father, Henry, knows all about it, is changing the time line a little to protect young Ricky? What if Ricky and he agreed to change the times to what they said and even the events? Saying there was another vehicle, even if they said they saw one at different times, would put a whole different thought and angle to a story, or to what actually happened."

"See, you think of so many angles. You should write a book. Of course, you would really have to change all the stories a little, or maybe a lot, if you were to write about all the cases you have had. That certainly would change things. But it doesn't change the fact that our best suspect is still Ricky, even with the stories they gave.

"We might as well be finished with the dog hair theory, I suppose. It's just not happening."

"I've never known you to give up like this, so close to having a conclusion on something, one way or the other. It seems you just have to wait until every bag is forensically investigated and every speck of dusk is clean, and every possible vehicle eliminated. You owe it to yourself on that one."

"You're right. Thank you for that reminder," Colton grinned at his deputy. "We have so many people pressuring us to find this killer, though, that this seems perfect. And, I have to admit that my theory with the dog hairs just hasn't panned out, and look at all the time and resources the department has given to that effort. I tried to keep just how much work has gone into that as quiet as possible, but you know how some things seems to leak out.

"We do have enough evidence to arrest Ricky for this, but my heart would really not be in it. True, he looks the part. But does long, scruffy hair, tattoos, and lack of a shower every now and then make a person a murderer?

"I saw you glance around the living room while we were at Ricky's place. There was no paraphernalia relating to drugs. In fact, I did not even see an ashtray. Come to think of it," he frowned, "there was not even the smell of cigarettes. I don't believe either of those young men smokes. They might even make their friends smoke outside, not allow smoking in the house. Maybe they are non-smokers."

This seemed a novel idea for two young men, but quite possible.

"What you are getting at," Eric said, "is that this would not be related to the fact that Ricky was high on drugs. He might be a drunk, even at that young age, but not a drug addict. However, things like this have happened when people have just been drunk on alcohol, no other drugs involved."

"I know," Colton responded, "and even an arrest, mug shots, fingerprints taken, would put this on his record. We checked him out when we returned that day. He does not even have a parking ticket! His record is squeaky clean. I think he is basically a good young man that has just lost his way. And I'm not so sure that doesn't have a lot to do with the father, Henry Carlton. His general attitude on life and the son were pretty negative. The young man certainly has no self-esteem from that angle. He's probably been told all this life that he's no good and won't amount to a hill of beans."

"He did tell us he was looking for a job, maybe that was the truth. What about your ability with the micro-expression stuff? I noticed you watched him carefully during the interview. Did it seem like he was lying about anything?"

"No, it didn't," Colton admitted, "but we also know there are those who can look you straight in the eye and lie with a straight face.

"If I'm wrong about this, and arrest this young man, how could I be responsible for putting this on his otherwise clean record? It would be there for future possible employers to find while considering him for a position, even if he explained that he was cleared of all charges. It's just simply *there,* in black and white, for anyone with a few dollars to see, from that point on and follows a person through life. We know there are employers who would not consider a person with that on the background, innocent or not."

He shook his head.

Eric sat quietly, letting his boss get all this off his chest. He knew Colton to be a good man, a fair man. He felt his dilemma.

But the decision was up to Colton. He *was* being pressured, unjustly, Eric thought, but still there it was. The good people of Dutch Mills were still so antsy about the whole situation, not to mention certain county officials and law enforcement from Fayetteville and across the line from Oklahoma.

He would make a bet that Lowe's and Walmart both were sold out of padlocks and deadbolts that went on doors and gates everywhere around there. Gun sales probably increased, with people thinking they needed extra protection, and it being fairly easy to buy guns in Arkansas.

Hell, Eric thought, *all they have to do is drive to Tulsa, to the gun show there at the fairgrounds and buy any gun, no background check or anything. Cash talks.*

"Can you come up with the gun?" Eric asked. "That's important. What if our thoughts are just that, and Henry Carlton goes to the linen drawer and brings out the old pistol from his youth? What then?"

Colton ran his fingers through his hair.

"It's all we've got. I'm going to go with it. Okay, just for you, I'll wait until all the bags have been cleared, which should be sometime this coming week. Then, I'm going to call the county prosecutor for an arrest warrant for Ricky Carlton, good, bad, or ugly."

"I know you do it with a heavy heart, but I won't blame you. It *is* all we've got and it's been too long, or so the public thinks."

They stood up. Colton walked over to the coffee bar, rinsed his cup, turned off the coffee pot and they left.

He hadn't even touched the fresh coffee.

Chapter 31

Jennifer walked into the lab on this Saturday morning wishing she were any place else. Since she was the very most junior member of the county forensic team, she was assigned the Saturday shift as long as this particular investigation was ongoing.

Jennifer was meticulous. If she were given this task, then she would complete it to the best of her ability.

She had earned a Bachelor of Science in Forensic Science from Indiana Wesleyan University, one of the best schools in the country for this type of thing. Not only had she graduated magna cum laude that year, but was the top student, academically, of her particular degree.

Wanting to spend a couple of years near her family, she applied for and was accepted for this position. Home was Westfork, a small community south of Fayetteville off Interstate 71. You used to have to go through the small town before the interstate was built between the Missouri line and Alma, on Interstate 40. Now, you had to exit off the Interstate.

She decided to stay close to home for two to three years before she applied to a more pressure-filled position at a large forensics lab. The experience with the Washington County Sheriff's Department would be invaluable experience for her and look good on her resume.

She hung her sweater in her designated place since it was now October and there was a chill in the air. It had been four months since this particular investigation started. She grinned when she thought about what the whole sheriff's department and the lab tech called it.

Operation Hair-brained. They all knew it was a take-off of the expression "hare-brained" after the story of The Tortoise and the Hare. They all felt like it was taking that long. This shifting through trash from people's cars looking for a hair or hairs from a particular type of dog, or actually a particular dog within the particular type of dog, was moving at a snail's pace.

But, wait a minute. She was mixing up her metaphors. It was either going at a snail's pace, or the pace of the tortoise.

She smiled at herself. Maybe both.

She stretched, reaching her hands in the air and wiggling her fingers before taking her place on a stool before the counter, which contained a state-of-the-art microscope with the latest technology. She expected to work on equipment here older than that at the university, but was pleasantly surprised when she saw the latest. This was just coming out when she graduated. There was no doubt Indiana Wesleyan had this by now.

A grant given to the sheriff's department allowed them to have this latest equipment. Jennifer didn't mind, of course, it was just something else to make her resume look better. She was nothing but ambitious, but had never let on to her fellow students. Her parents knew of her plans; they were just grateful she wanted to stay close to the family for a while.

Unfortunately, the bags of evidence the various teams of men had collected from the many cars they had to search and vacuum were not in order. There was a reason for this. The men had only put numbers on them, to be cross-referenced later with names of the people, or other information. Some sort of privacy issue. They thought the number was enough.

Last week, another lab tech had stumbled and unfortunately fell into the folding table that was completely covered with the brown paper bags. They had gone off the table to scatter over the floor everywhere. Jennifer and the other tech had quickly picked them up and placed them back on the table, but there was no telling what order they had been in to begin with and in what order they went back on the table. Each team had numbered theirs separately. There could be three of the same number at any given time.

They were to report directly to Sheriff Colton if anything was discovered. They reported twice a week regularly with negative reports.

This morning, she had only six bags left to process.

She sterilized the counter in front of her. Then, after "making her nest," as she referred to it, in her regular position, she reached for the nearest bag. She carefully dumped the contents onto the counter, ever so slowly, keeping the dust level as low as possible.

She saw some of the same "junk" she had seen in all the other bags that had come her way. There were pebbles, gravel, dust, "dreck" of all sorts, and, yes, even hairs of some sort. These would be human, cat, dog, or whatever animal the person had allowed inside the vehicle.

There had been ferret, gerbil, rabbit, and other non-domesticated animal hairs and even bits of feces in the messes she had processed thus far. She assumed these animals were considered "pets" by these owners, but she didn't. They had either just bought them, taking them to the vet, or taking them away.

Whatever.

She was taught that people did weird things with weird animals at times. Nothing would surprise her at this point. A bit of snakeskin in a vehicle or two was not a shock.

But, so far, no matching dog hairs.

They were not allowed to listen to music as they worked. They lab manager considered that too much of a distraction, so she hummed to herself as she worked. Never once, though, was she distracted. She would give these last six bags the same attention as the other hundred or so she had worked on. This was not to mention the fact that the other lab tech that usually worked with her had also processed hundreds of bags.

There really were a lot of people who lived out in the countryside. There were more houses you did not see than you could see just from the highways.

Sorting the stuff on the counter took the longest time, then she was ready to begin testing. She always started with the hairs first, since that was the emphasis.

The first were dog hairs but did not match the murdered dog. Yes, she considered the poor dog as murdered. He didn't deserve a death like that anymore than the woman did.

"Whoa!" she said out loud after she had placed the last hair under the microscope, side by side with one from the slain dog.

"I can't believe this!" she was talking to herself, but that didn't matter.

She checked several more times just to be sure of what she was seeing.

She leaned back. She discovered she was shaking.

She had just found a match to the slain dog! She knew she would be asked if she were sure, and she was. She knew her job.

She leaned back on her stool. She stepped off it, ever so slowly. She did not want to disturb a thing on the counter in front of her.

"Jay, come here.! Quickly!" she said to the other lab tech. He was hunched over a counter several rows front of her, sitting on a stool.

He heard the urgency and excitement in her voice, but he was at a critical point at one of his own tests.

"You'll have to wait for just a minute," he responded. "I hear how excited you are, but I can't leave this right now. What is it?"

"I can't tell you, you'll just have to see for yourself."

Jennifer had to just sit there, shaking, while he finished what he was doing.

He twirled around suddenly on his stool, facing her.

"Okay, what is it? The long, lost dog hair we are so diligently searching for?" He said it in a teasing voice, not expecting the answer he was about to receive.

"As a matter of a fact, yes, I found a hair that is a perfect match to the little guy that was murdered."

Jay quickly stood up and walked around the counter to her.

"Well, why didn't you say so?"

"I tried. I started to, but you told me to wait for you to finish. Did you also find one, is that why your test was so much more important than mine?"

"Of course not. I didn't think there would be two vehicles with the same dog hair, did you?"

All the while he was talking, Jennifer took even another step backward so he could take her place on the stool to peer into the microscope. He didn't touch a thing, of course, just put his eye to the scope. He also knew to move slowly and deliberately.

He saw the hair from the dead dog, which had been specially labeled. It was treated with "kid gloves" every time either of them wanted to compare hairs. Jennifer had just reached that point with her bag right now, while Jay was still sifting through his dust and other debris.

He looked up, shaking his head.

"You did it, kid, you really did. That makes the two of us to verify this and sign that this is the identical match. You'd better leave this just like it is and call Sheriff Colton.

I don't care that it's Saturday or what time it is. He certainly won't want to miss this."

Suddenly Jay slid off the stool, grabbed Jennifer, and started dancing around the laboratory with her, but away from that counter. They were both on a high, the kind that a job well done, achieving the required, but unexpected results, gives a person.

They were giddy and laughing when they stopped. For some reason, Jay had started singing "Stand by Me," the old song by Ben E. King as they moved about the room, making sure they were well aware from the microscope.

She was still shaking.

"We do need to stand by each other with this thing. What a find!"

She left his arms and walked to the counter across the room. The telephone was on the counter. Opening a drawer under the telephone, she found the piece of paper that Sheriff Colton had written his private cell number on.

Her hands were still shaking as she punched in the number. Although it was Saturday, he had, multiple times, emphasized the fact they were to call him personally, anytime, if and when they found something.

Something was not the word to use here.

This was *it*.

The "hair-brained scheme" had worked.

And she had found it.

Chapter 32

Marsha had a hard time this Saturday morning keeping Colton busy. He was very restless. She knew the Dutch Mills murder was eating him alive. She needed to find something for him to do.

By mid-morning she had him raking leaves with her. Most of the leaves were from a huge oak tree in the front yard. When they saw this place almost two years ago, the first thing that caught their eye was this huge tree. They looked at each other and at the same time had mouthed "leaves." Which meant a lot of work to rake them, of course.

But that didn't matter. They not only fell in love with the yard and this tree in the yard, but the house plan was ideal for their family needs. They did not look any further. They told the real estate agent they would take it.

Today, raking the leaves was helping him relax. More and more leaves fell gently around them, and they laughed that it was a never-ending battle.

After raking a large pile in the center of the yard, they decided it was time to take a break. They went to the back of the house, to the sunroom, that housed several chairs and a table. Marchs went in for some coffee. She blended her own.

"Good coffee," Colton said. He held up the cup toward her.

"Thank you, sir," she returned.

"But not as good as Miss Maggie's. You have to understand that, of course." Colton smiled at his wife. He was teasing her.

"Of course," she laughed.

Miss Maggie was a woman who ran the only "gas station," as she called it, in Hogeye, Arkansas.

Not only had this been the ideal house for them, but Colton found they were located in an ideal spot for the Washington County Sheriff, whoever that might have been. Although Colton had driven many of the roads in his county when he first came, it was later, during this case at Dutch Mills, that he discovered a county road that went through Hogeye, Arkansas, going to Prairie Grove. It was not on any map. This enabled him to miss going up to Fayetteville, turning west on Highway 62 and having to go through the City of Farmington.

Eric always met him in Prairie Grove and they went west from there. It had saved much time during their interviews and vacuumings of the vehicles of the group of homeowners he had assigned to himself and Eric, the group that was around Dutch Mills.

The residents of Hogeye were so used to him driving through now that they waved at him. One time, early on during his travels, he decided to stop at the one and only convenience store to fill his coffee cup. He expected the coffee to be awful, coming from such a small place, but he needed some. To his surprise, it was very good. He complimented the middle-aged woman behind the counter, who confessed that it was her special blend. She seemed very pleased that the county sheriff liked it, and wanted to give it to him free. He insisted, however, that he pay for it, because he would certainly be stopping for more.

Every time now, when he went through Hogeye, which seemed to be quite often, he stopped for Miss Maggie's coffee. Several residents were usually there now. They wanted to chat for a few minutes. They didn't keep him long, of course, but just the fact that they felt they now personally knew the sheriff made them feel more secure.

They confessed that this Dutch Mills thing still had them on edge. They started locking their doors here at night, even their barns, because of this murder. After all, Hogeye wasn't *that* far from Dutch Mills. The guy might be anywhere.

Colton agreed and told them that it was good to take every precaution.

That was the reference now with Marsha. She and Maggie both were neck-to-neck in popularity with their coffee blends. Marsha didn't mind that Colton thought that. She realized how important it would be to the woman to think that hers was the favorite of the sheriff.

They were quietly sipping their coffee when the phone rang. Colton had two phones on the table that he kept with him at all times. One was the official department phone, but on Saturdays that transferred to the station house, where the dispatcher took care of whatever it was. Any calls on the weekends usually did not involve Colton. The rest of the unit could handle them.

He looked up at Marsha when he realized it was his private phone that lit up. Probably Abby. Marsha's phone was probably still connected to the charger by her bed. She was bad about not carrying it with her. They would not hear it ring where they were.

He frowned. Why would Abby call? She always sent a text.

He picked up the phone.

"It's the forensics lab," he said to Marsha. He was so startled he had not answered it.

"Well, answer it, before it quits ringing," she said. She smiled.

Colton answered on the second ring. He remembered he told them to call him anytime if they found something important in the Dutch Mills case. Everything was important to Colton, for any case, and there were several more ongoing right now, but this was one had top priority. He didn't give out this number lightly.

He had to admit later, though, that his mind had been entirely on something else, not the murder at Dutch Mills, when this call came through.

It was late October, so they had the windows open in the sunroom. A gentle, cooling breeze came through the windows, ruffling the curtains Marsha had made especially for these windows. It really was his favorite room of the house. He was glad they had found a house they liked with this particular feature.

He could smell the pot roast cooking in the slow cooker and was looking forward to a relaxing dinner with his wife. The three boys had all gone three different ways with friends, with two of them planning to spend the night with their buds. The other one would not be home until 10:00 p.m.

He had to admit they were all good kids, always letting them know where they were and who they were with. They came home when they were told to, usually about five minutes before the time required.

Colton laughed and said they knew how to play "the parent game."

"Hello? Sheriff Colton Mitchell here."

"Sheriff, Sheriff!" came the breathless, excited voice.

Oh, no, thought Colton. *What now?* He had never talked to Jennifer, so he didn't recognize the voice.

"I found it, honest, I really did!"

She was so excited, she forgot to identify herself.

"Who is this, and what did you find?" Colton asked.

"Oh, I'm sorry. This is Jennifer Guthrie. I'm a tech at the forensics lab. Sheriff, I just found a dog hair that matches the one you took from the murdered dog at Dutch Mills."

"What? *What?*"

He gave the common reaction. She was not offended. Everyone said this at first when they were waiting for important information. It was like they really were not expecting to find what they were looking for.

Colton nearly dropped his phone. His cup of coffee was still in his other hand. He started shaking at this news. He straightened up in his chair and nearly spilled his coffee as he sat it on the table beside him.

"Are you sure?" He couldn't believe it.

Marsha had gone into the house but came out to listen. By his tone, she realized this was something important.

"Yes, I'm positive, really I am. I would be willing to go to Court and testify that this is the identical hair from that particular dog. We are required to always have two of us in the lab at all times, probably as much to do with security as anything, but, Jay, the other tech, came to look. He will verify it and sign for it. We have no doubt, but I'll let my director see if you want triple proof. We have to work in pairs here at the lab and I've already had my colleague look at it."

She repeated herself about Jay because she was so excited. She wanted him to believe her.

"He agrees with me and is just as excited. Oh, Sheriff, it was in one of the last six bags I was to process. It was even the last dog hair in that particular bag. I know how long you've waited for this."

She didn't add that she was also sure he didn't believe his theory would work, but she had heard how thorough he was, checking out things other people might not even think of.

"You know the protocol for preserving it, of course."

"Of course," she answered. "But I thought you might want to look into the microscope yourself and see for yourself. We can keep it in place until you get here. We probably won't even breath, we are so excited. There's no way this will be contaminated, or thrown out as evidence. We have him!"

Chapter 33

You're right, of course. I wasn't thinking. Of course, I want to see it, to verify it, also. I'll call Eric, my chief deputy, to meet me there, too. He'll want to see it with his own eyes, also. I'll be right there. Stay there."

"Of course," she answered. Where did he expect her to go?

Nothing could happen to this!

Marsha had heard Colton's exclamation and the clatter of the cup on the table. She leaned on the door frame from the kitchen as she listened to his part of the conversation.

He looked up at her.

"You won't believe this. That was a forensics lab tech. She identified one of the dog hairs from one of the bags collected at one of the homes around Dutch Mills. It exactly matches the murdered dog.

"We have him, we have him!"

He rose and gathered her into his arms. He held her away from him.

"So, your 'hair-brained theory' worked," she said.

He seemed surprised. He laughed.

"You know about that?"

"Yes, I know about that. At the grill party at Allison's house, we ladies talked about it. Gary had told her, I suppose. I never mentioned it to you that I knew. I didn't want to make you feel even worse than I knew you were as this investigation seemed to be going nowhere."

"Yes, now, maybe, I'll be vindicated. You know these feelings of mine always seem to work out, somehow."

"Yes, but I was just beginning to worry about this one, though."

"I have to go to the lab. Right now."

"Of course, you do," she responded.

He was already turning toward the kitchen door. She followed him as he went through the kitchen and into the mudroom between the kitchen and the garage. She watched as he collected his gun belt off the hook he always put it on when he came home.

It was the last of eight hooks, those containing various caps, jackets, keys. On the floor below that were several pairs of shoes and boots, both his, hers and the kids. This was a mudroom in the true definition of a mudroom. It was large enough to contain a shower stall and other toilet facilities. The shower here had been a godsend for the boys after various sports. They left their dirty clothes in a hamper here, their cleats on the floor to be cleaned outside later.

They had been lucky to find his house with this room, also. He had used the shower many times after fighting rain, mud, whatever, on the job. It kept Marsha as happy as it kept the house clean.

She watched as he put the belt around him and gave it a final hitch. He took his hat off a hook.

He turned toward her, as he always did when he was leaving. He smiled as she smiled at him.

"I'll see you when I see you," he said.

"Yes, I know," she answered.

"I love you," he said, as he always did.

"And I love you back, but more," she responded, as she always did.

They smiled at each other.

This was their routine. Each understood, but never spoke of it, that each time Colton left the house in the call of duty, that it might be the last time he left. He might not return. That was the nature of the job, the nature of this beast.

So, they made a habit of saying "I love you," never leaving the house with any sort of angry words or thoughts between them.

Life was too precious for that.

As he went through the garage to his cruiser, which was parked in backwards, she went to the living room to look out of the large bay window there. From there she had a perfect view of his car as he pulled out of the garage.

He always waved on good days like this and she waved back. On rainy days, he flashed his lights in a final "see you later" gesture.

She turned back to the kitchen as he pulled out into the street in the direction of the forensics lab.

She went straight to the slow cooker and turned it down to "low" to let the roast inside cook at a slower rate. She might even have to turn it down later to "keep warm."

Whichever, the meal would be ready when Colton returned, however late.

Yes, she had heard how the men had called his plan the "hair-brained theory," after the story of the tortoise and the hare. What they didn't realize was that he really was her "tortoise," ever faithful, plodding right along in his steady, unstoppable way when he started a case, nothing but thorough in every detail he could think of.

And that way with the family.

Her tortoise.

Steady.

Unstoppable.

Winning the day.

As usual.

This would be no exception.

She knew it.

Again, it was the nature of her beast.

She picked up a book and went to sit in his chair in the sunroom.

She knew her husband was good, but this would prove how good. She never said a word to him, but she, too, had heard from some of the wives of the deputies what his theory had been called, and sometimes it was worse than "hair-brained."

Only she knew the full anguish Colton felt in not being able to find this killer. Four months and a little! If anyone could take it to the end and find the killer, Colton could.

She said a little prayer for him.

As usual.

Chapter 34

Colton immediately called Eric to meet him at the lab. He was waiting by the time Colton pulled up. He did not live far and had been home when Colton called.

They were glad to meet Jennifer and Jay.

"Where is it?" Colton asked. They could tell how excited he was.

Jennifer led the way to the microscope.

"Careful," she warned.

Both men looked at her. She blushed.

"Sorry, it's a habit, I'm afraid. All lab techs feel the need to tell others to be careful around the equipment and evidence and such. Sorry, again."

Colton smiled at her. "That's fine, Jennifer, but don't worry. As excited as we are, we will be extra careful."

Colton slowly and carefully put his eye to the microscope. He placed his hands behind his back so there could be no accident with them. He looked back and forth several times at each slide.

He rose up.

"Wow! They're identical, all right. I can't believe it. Your turn, Eric."

Eric repeated the same procedure. He rose up and backed away.

"Incredible, just incredible. What's the number on the bag?"

Jennifer picked up the bag and turned it around.

Eric recognized his handwriting on the bag, so it had to be one from the houses they went to.

"Number 37," she said.

Colton looked at Eric.

"That puts it about three-fourths way through the houses we went to, doesn't it? Didn't we do about fifty, in all?"

"Fifty-one, if you want to be exact, but who's counting? Right?" Eric smiled at Colton.

They had painstakingly counted every house.

"I certainly don't remember which number went with which house. We'll have to crosscheck the number on the computer. Nancy has done such an amazing job of cross-referencing numbers and names and addresses, vehicle colors and types and any other way she could think of. We'll be able to find out the name quickly. Now, let's get that bagged under correct procedure and we'll take it."

Nancy was one of the sheriff's deputies assigned to office duties after being in a slight accident. She was unable to go on patrol for a while, but she had shown an incredible ability for organization.

"I'm not about to have any hotshot attorney try to say the evidence was tainted or tampered with," Colton said.

"I hear that," Eric agreed.

Under the watchful eyes of the other three, Jennifer secured the slide by procedure. She prepared the paperwork to transfer the evidence from the lab to the sheriff's department. Both lab techs signed off on it, as well as Colton and Eric on their end.

Both men just stared at the bag for a moment.

Colton frowned. The number seemed so familiar, but he couldn't place it exactly to the name or house that corresponded with it. He felt he should be able to, but after a time, they all seemed to blur together.

After all, in the past almost four months, this case, although it was the biggest and most important for the department, had not been the only one they had worked on.

There were the usual B&E's, domestic disputes, several major altercations at The Oasis and Jake's Watering Hole, two "lounges," or so they called themselves, that were located between Fayetteville and the next town, Farmington on State Highway 67 West. There was about a three-mile stretch in there that belonged to the county. That meant the two bars, or so Colton called them, belonged to him and his men.

There seemed to be more and more confrontations between individual people in various places. The general population was so stressed that nerves became frayed at the drop of a hat. There were the usual accidents on the highways and Interstate in areas that were in the jurisdiction of the county or he assisted with.

Along with all those, the teams of two went to the interviews and car vacuumings as they could. That's why it had taken these four months to complete this part of the investigation.

He looked over at Eric.

"Remember who this is?" he asked.

Eric shook his head. "I should, I know. The number seems so familiar, but I just can't place it. Sorry. There just were so many."

"I know. That's okay, we'll find out at the office."

Colton told Jennifer to complete the last bags, but he knew he had his answer. It was just a matter now of finding out which name this number went with, where they lived and that would be on the map in his office.

After complimenting the techs on what a great job they had done all the way through the investigation, and especially Jennifer, they left.

Eric followed him back to the office.

Chapter 35

The three officers on duty in the building were surprised to see them come in. They always had a dispatcher, an officer on desk duty, and an officer assigned to file the past week's paperwork on duty at any time in the building, and especially on weekends. This was for security reasons as well as serving the county. They would call in others if needed.

They noticed the brown paper sack Colton carried as they greeted the officers. They looked at each other when the two men passed by.

Doughnuts? This must be serious. They looked at each other a second time when the two men went into the office and closed the door.

They shrugged and went back to their duties. They would hear soon enough what it was all about.

The first thing Colton did was go to the three file cabinets on one wall of his office. He pulled out the third drawer down. He knew this drawer was only half full. He put the brown paper sack in the back and closed the drawer.

"Why put it there?" Eric asked. "Is that a secure enough place to leave something so important? In fact, it's the only evidence we have."

"To hide it in plain sight. No one will think to look for it there, if anyone were going to. As far as I know, no one touches my files but me. Everything anyone needs is in the file room. Right?"

"You're right, of course," Eric responded. "Good idea."

Colton was nothing if not thorough. Maybe too detailed at times, but in this case, he was glad he had turned the job of cross-referencing names and addresses, vehicle types, telephone numbers, whatever he could think of to identify each homeowner to Nancy.

Eric pulled up a chair around the desk to look at the monitor as Colton typed in the number.

The spaces filled in.

Colton straightened up and pushed his chair back.

"Well, I'll be damned! You're kidding me!" he exclaimed. He looked over at Eric, who had been with him when they interviewed this man, as he had been with Colton for all of them.

"Recognize who that is? That address?"

"I just can't remember. Sorry. Who is it?"

"It's the old man down the pig-trail down the end of the first pig-trail, the one we had to walk about a mile to get to the house out in the boonies. Remember now?"

"Of course," his deputy answered, "but he seemed like such a nice old man, so open about everything. I can't believe he would kill like that."

"Well, that's where the matching dog hair comes from," Colton responded. "His car. Unfortunately, it's too late to go out there this evening."

He looked out the office window to the west, where the sun was just ready to go below the tree line on the horizon.

"There's no use heading out that way right now. By the time we arrived at the mailbox, it would be dark. There's no way I'm going to walk into that woods after dark. Besides, he would hear us coming and really bring out the shotgun!"

"You're right, of course, it's just going to be so hard waiting for morning. I probably won't sleep a wink. You should hear Mary fussing at me, when I get up during the night because I'm thinking too hard on a case. On this case, though, it would be different."

She would understand, just like all the wives did. Every once in a while, of course, a wife just could not deal with the requirements for a deputy's job. Then, inevitably, a divorce would occur. It just couldn't be helped. Not every woman could handle the stress of saying good-bye to her husband as he walked out the door, not knowing if he would return, and that at all hours. There were the usual suspicions of them being elsewhere other than on the job, and other questions.

"Is that general warrant still in effect, in case we need it? We won't arrest anyone tomorrow, just ask some more questions about his car and where he's been, who he's visited, that sort of thing. There's going to be a lot more here, I can feel it."

Eric looked at a copy of the warrant.

"Well, we're lucky. We have a week to go on this one. That should give us plenty of time to work all this out. I still can't believe the old man could do such a thing. Besides, what's the connection to an old man out in the boonies and the pastor's wife? It just doesn't make sense."

"You always 'feel' right," Eric said. He was already planning on how the guys would apologize for doubting Colton, for the "hair-brained theory."

Who had first thought of that, anyway? He couldn't remember, just that it had come out of that first meeting, that first Monday after the murder.

It seemed so long ago.

Colton looked at the clock on the wall.

"It's getting dark outside. I'll pick you up at eight in the morning and we'll go out then, okay?"

"Sure, but I know neither of us will get any sleep to-night. This is just too important, too exciting."

"You're right there, but by the time we would get down there this evening, it would be dark. No use facing the business end of a shotgun. Van did not have a phone, re-member? There's no number here in the computer. He has to see us coming."

Colton didn't realize, in his excitement, that he was re-peating himself.

"According to the info here, we went there about two and a half months ago. Remember, we decided to talk to those on the western edge of our assigned territory, going south, then come north and work our way up to Dutch Mills, after the stop at the Carltons in between that sched-ule. At the time we thought we were pretty organized. Maybe there could have been a better way.

"That brings up another interesting question. Why was the lab tech just now getting to his bag? Shouldn't that bag have been checked several weeks ago?"

He wasn't aware of the accident and mess with the bags, of course.

"I'm sure they had their methods. I'm just happy it's done, now," Eric answered.

"You're right. No worries now."

Chapter 36

For the third time in the last two years, Colton was down at the end of the pig-trail at the mailbox with another pig-trail to go. He thought sarcastically that it must be his destiny to end up in this spot. At least this was October and it would be much cooler walking the mile down the lane to Van's house.

They locked the Range Rover and started walking down the lane. This could only be called a lane, although one car could go down it. Grass grew up in the middle of the road. Last time the grass was tall, full, now it was dying off for the season.

"I wish Van had a phone," Eric began. "This is Sunday morning and we have no way of knowing if Van goes to church somewhere and, if so, then at what time. We may be waiting for him for quite a while."

"You know he explained last time about being in a dead zone, with no cell phone reception. I can believe it. Remember the woman at that one house on Arkansas Highway 244 that also said she could not get cell phone reception, the one who owned property to the Oklahoma line? She said there was a ghost, that AT&T seemed to know just where the state line was, and even if you were talking, coming from the west, the phones just went dead at the line. Deader than a doornail, as she put it. She understood, of course, that it was just the lay of the land, there was actually a cell tower about three miles away to the north."

Colton looked over at Eric.

"You remember Carlton griping about Jones having the cell tower on the hill at his property, just barely in Arkansas, because the Jones property went to the line?"

Eric nodded. He remembered.

"Just a strange geological arrangement of a small knoll on that ridge, right there as you go into Arkansas, it's the continuation of the ridge that runs through Dutch Mills, really along the Arkansas/Oklahoma line until it meets up with the Boston Mountains at the Southwest corner of Washington County, but it means no cell phone reception at the house. Of course, they had a land-line, one which the mother had since 1969 when she moved there. It was still on the wall, still little holes that you put your fingers in and dialed around until you stopped at that little metal tab, then you let it go. She said her mother left it there on the wall by the kitchen because as long as it was installed that way, the telephone company serviced it because it was their equipment and telephone. They had come out several times over the years to service it, no charge to the mom. The mom's reasoning was "if it ain't broke, don't fix it," and it stayed repaired. She could make local and long distance calls from it, so that was all she needed. That took care of any extra phone bills, the bill was only around $25 a month, even up to the time she passed away a few years ago.

"She said the mom never complained, though, because she knew for sure, over the years, that the knoll had made several tornadoes pull back up when they got there, so they missed the house. The mom swore that she heard them pass over the house up in the air, it was just that the last one, that destroyed the original place, had come directly from the south, totally jumping over that white house across the highway and doing enough damage that the mom's house had to be replaced."

"That could be meteorologically true," Eric responded. "I've heard of that because, as you say, of the lay of the land. Tornadoes have a tendency to pull back into the air like that at times when they encounter certain land masses. But I think if a tornado wants you, it will get you, no matter what."

Colton continued.

"The woman complained that they still had to drive the three-quarters of a mile up to Highway 59, park in the extra space there, to use their cell phone. They had replaced the old dial phone with one on the counter, still had the same number, realized they needed it for 911 purposes, since the cell phone didn't work in just that spot."

"I wonder if the house across the street was in the same dead zone?"

They were just chatting to make the mile walk to Van's go faster but fell silent.

Eric looked around. This was a different time of the year than their previous visit. Now, the leaves on the trees lining this lane were beautiful, having changed colors for autumn. The maples took on all their glorious oranges, reds, yellows, while at the same time retaining some of the green leaves. The sumac, which he had always called "poison sumac," had changed to deep purples. Leaves slowly drifted down around them. The sun was behind them and it shimmered off the leaves in front of them. The sun especially made the silver-leafed maples shimmer and glitter as a gentle breeze turned the leaves first one way and then another.

On one side of the lane was an old fence with wooden fence posts. Eric could tell the age because it was an old-style barbed wire, with three strands connecting the boards. In a couple of places the fence posts had rotted and the barbed wire was on the ground. Obviously, if the owner who put up the fence had cattle or whatever in the past, it was in the distant past. It had taken many, many years for the fence to reach this stage.

He knew there were museums with all types and styles of barbed-wire displayed in them. He knew they would like to have some of this. But whether this fence and the land beyond it belonged to Van, that was another question. Maybe he would ask him.

It could be that this was just an access road to his property. By law, if someone else had your property "land-locked," they had to provide access to your place. That would stand to reason since this was such a narrow lane. The county would have provided the access to the mail-box, with other means provided for this passage.

All in all, this walk was very pleasant. The weather was just right, not too warm and not too cool. This was really a Norman Rockwell-type setting.

Perfect Americana.

It was just too bad they might discover some unpleasant results at the end of it.

And they were just about there.

They heard dogs barking, which suddenly appeared ahead. They were guarding the yard and house but did not venture down this lane too far toward the men.

Obviously, Van had rescued the two dogs he had talked about previously.

Drawn by the barking of the dogs, Van also appeared in the middle of the lane. They were about two hundred yards from the front yard of the house.

Van raised his hand in greeting. He hushed the dogs and waited until the men were within talking distance.

"That's a right pleasant walk this time of year, isn't it? Do it every day going to the mailbox. Do it in the summer, too, it just isn't as nice. Figure it's good exercise for me.

Got to keep moving, you know. Didn't expect to see you gentlemen again."

This last he said as he held out his hand to shake first Colton's, then Eric's hands.

They shook hands. They didn't sense any evil or meanness in this man.

"Come on and sit down. How about some lemonade? I squeeze the lemons myself. It's always been my favorite drink. My wife used to keep some around all the time. She squeezed the lemons for fresh juice, so I guess I just continued doing it. Nothing else seems to taste just right. I'm glad she showed me once how much sugar she puts in it, or I would have had a hard time coming up with the right amount. I'll just be a few minutes."

Colton and Eric sat down in the metal chairs that formed a semi-circle on the lawn. One was red, and one was yellow. They were faded. They had seen their better days, but still as comfortable as that type of chair could be. It was pleasant in the yard with a large shade tree above them.

Obviously, Van had visitors on occasion since the chairs were in this configuration, with a small round table in the middle, used for drinks.

They looked around. The same old rusty pickup was parked in the same place. Closer to the house, because it was probably used more often, was the same 2008 Toyota Corolla, whitish, sort of, in color. It was more the color described on the paperwork, but Colton thought it could very well have appeared "whitish" in a heavy rain down at the end of a road.

In a few minutes, Van was back with tall glasses of lemonade, not much ice. They both took a drink. It was just right, which they told Van.

He said once again that it was his wife's fault. He laughed.

"Now, fellows, what can I help you with this time?

"We need to ask you some more questions pertaining to the matter we were here about before. Mainly, we need to have more details on your car."

"Cory?" he asked. "What about it? Pretty good car, considering."

Obviously, he was one of those people who name their vehicles.

"Considering what?" Colton asked.

"Well, you never know what you're getting when you buy a used car, you know. But I'd heard good things from several people, or at least the men from the Co-op in Stilwell, that King Motors there in Farmington usually had pretty good vehicles, so that's why I bought it from there. I've been pleased that the motor didn't start knocking after a week, like maybe they had put some STP or something in the oil to help soothe out any pings or pongs in the engine. I've heard of that happening many times with vehicles you buy from used car lots. Keeps the motor sounding good just long enough that, by law, the dealer is no longer responsible to do anything about it. And it could be something seriously wrong with the engine, or something else expensive.

"They told me they put a new alternator in it, so that was okay. Otherwise, it sounded okay to me."

He thought they wanted to know all about the car. All this information did startle them. For some reason, they both thought Van had owned the car since 2008, the original date. The license plate was sure old enough. Everything must have checked out with the officer that was put in charge of background checks on the vehicles in this case. He never mentioned otherwise.

"Just when did you buy the Toyota from King Motors?" Eric asked.

"Oh, it must have been…oh…let me think. A couple of months ago, it was. Just a minute and I'll think of the exact date."

Colton found himself holding his breath. He let it out slowly. He looked over at Eric, who was looking at him. Eric raised his eyebrows, silently sending a question to Colton.

"Had to be the middle of August, I'd say," he said. "Wait!"

He jumped up and hurried toward the house before either of them could say anything.

"Paperwork?" Eric asked.

"Oh, I do hope so," Colton returned. "This may be the break we need. And to have found the dog hair there. This is traceable evidence. Very traceable."

Both men could hardly wait until the man returned.

Sure enough, Van had several pieces of paper in his hands.

"You can look at all these, if you like," he said. He handed them to Colton.

Colton's hands shook as he took them.

He found the date he was looking for.

"You purchased this vehicle from King Motors on August 10th."

"Yeah, I knew it was somewhere around the middle of August. Pretty hot, it was, but I still looked at every vehicle on that lot. Had to buy something. A friend took me there and I told him to let me off and leave, that I wasn't leaving the car lot until I bought something. I figured that way, it made me buy something. Else, I might have had a tendency to put it off. But, Old Blue there…"

He pointed toward the pickup, which by now was a faded blue.

"…needs a rest. I figure I'll just drive him around the place, is all, not out in the traffic."

Both men looked puzzled. They looked around the yard.

Van laughed. He knew what they were thinking.

"No, I don't drive him around and around in circles in this yard." He laughed. "You can't see the road from this side of the house, but see that driveway going behind the house over there?"

He pointed to the side of the house were the pickup sat off to the side of a well-worn drive. They nodded.

"That takes you to the back gate, that leads to the barn and my fields beyond that. Got myself about twenty head of cattle back there. Also, got a good hay field. Just mowed and baled the last hay of the season a few weeks ago. Old Blue sure comes in handy for that. Usually bale enough to last the cows through the winter, along with some feed I buy from the Co-op, but I try to keep my expenses down as best I can. Nothing's cheap these days."

Now, why didn't we know there was more to this man than meets the eye? Colton thought.

Eric couldn't stand it any longer. He wanted to know about the barbed wire, although he knew it was putting off some serious business.

"Do you own the property coming down the lane to your house? The side with the old fence along it?"

"Why, yes, as a matter of a fact, I do. That fence is old. It was there when I bought the property. About twenty years ago, I decided to put a fence from that corner there," he began, pointing, "to about a half mile south where it meets another corner. That way, I just eliminated that part of the pasture. I know it's overgrown now, but I just don't need it, anymore. Can't handle more than the twenty head I have right now and the hay to feed them. I have an old hay baler, one that puts out the rectangle bales. Can't afford one of those new round balers. That's really big bucks. One of my sons and his son come from Fayetteville to help me when I need work done on the place, including mowing and baling the hay, putting it up in the barn. Want to see the barn?" Van asked.

"Sure," Colton said. They stood up.

If this was just something to put them off, hoping they would forget what they were here for, it wouldn't work. Colton just thought it was interesting.

As they walked around the house, Eric asked about the barbed wire.

"Yep, probably is a collector's item. I saw on the Internet how they collect that stuff. If anyone from one of those museums ever discovers me out this way, I'd probably give them some. Got to find me first, though."

He laughed. Then, he started talking about the various types of barbed wire. Eric knew he was out of his league on this subject. Van had vast experience with stringing fences.

"Just how does your son know when you need him? Didn't you tell us you're in a dead zone for cell phones?"

"Skype," Van answered.

Colton and Eric were walking a few steps behind the old man. They looked at each other, with each managing to keep a straight face.

"Of course," Colton said.

Yep, certainly more to Van than we will ever know, he thought.

Again, he pointed. They looked that way.

The barn was a neat as the front yard of the house. They could see a few of the cattle when Van pointed them out in a field. The rest must be further away.

"I usually have enough hay to sell about a thousand bales. I have some regular guys that buy it every year. I sow good seed, keep the weeds out. It brings in some extra income. Now, in case you gentleman are wondering, if I make over the amount I can legally make with my Social Security, I file a tax form for that year. I keep it legal."

They wondered at one point when they left here the first time how the man made a living. Now, they knew.

This amount of cleared land, fenced, the hay crop, room for much more cattle, all this equipment, the size and condition of the barn, the house. Van Hattabaugh might not have a lot of *liquid* assets, right at this moment in time, but he was sitting on a fortune.

Colton suspected the old man knew it.

They went back to the chairs and the paperwork.

"How long have you had that license plate?" Colton asked.

"At least twenty years, maybe more. I'm sure glad Arkansas lets you keep the same license number from year to year, even the same plate, if it stays in good shape. I can't keep up with my Social Security number, I would be lost trying to memorize a new license plate number every year."

Colton thought it looked like it was time to get a new plate, not just a new tag. He didn't say so, though. A lot of things were starting to fall into place.

"And when did you get your new 2016 tag?"

"Went the same afternoon I bought the car, stopped by the tag office in Lincoln. I had all my property taxes paid up, so it just took a few minutes to get everything taken care of."

The old man was also very sharp.

"Just why do you guys need more info about the Corolla?" he asked.

"There have been some new developments on that case. We are just checking several vehicles a second time."

"Bet it has something to do with those dog hairs!"

Van cackled, throwing his head back.

He thought he was being funny. It was a good thing he did not look at the two men, though, or he would have seen the telltale, startled looks on their faces. Why would he have said something like that?

"Just an angle we have to investigate," Colton said. "You said you only own a shotgun, no rifles, or pistols, or other type guns?"

"Nope, just the one shotgun I told you about. Do you need to see it, too, like the car?"

"No, that won't be necessary."

They stood up.

"We need to go. Thanks for your help."

It seems Van needed to talk more. He walked with them back down the lane. That was okay with Eric. The man talked more about the fence and history of barbed wire. They parted about halfway back.

Colton and Eric were quiet until they got back into the Range Rover. Eric had taken notes of the dates the car was purchased and a few other details. He flipped open his notepad.

"We missed that by just a few days. A few days! Can you believe it? And, no, we didn't ask him how long he had owned that car. By the looks of it at the time, as it still looks now, and the look of the license plate, I just assumed he had owned it for years."

Eric grinned. "You know what they say about the word assume."

"Do I ever, especially now. You know this means the dog hair was in the car from the car dealer. What? King Motors, in Farmington. It might mean they didn't even vacuum the car when it came in, or a number of other things."

Colton could kick himself.

All this time.

"That's for us to find out," Eric replied. "You have to admit the investigation is just now getting interesting. Just getting started."

"I don't think Van is the killer," Eric said.

"No, I don't, either. I wonder just *where* this will lead us," Colton said. "Next stop, King Motors. We have enough time today to get there."

It was late in the day. They'd spent a long time at Van Hattabaugh's house, but it had certainly been worth it. Not only had it been worth it with this case, but Colton would never judge another person in another house in the country as being poor and having to live there because he, she, or they had to, economically.

People made all kinds of choices based on a number of reasons.

They were on their way back.

In more ways than one.

Chapter 37

They were just as disappointed when they pulled in front of the office at King Motors as they had been excited to get there.

The only thing on the lot were the used cars, neatly lined up in two rows, each one declaring what a deal it was. Some had prices posted, some did not. Otherwise, the place was deserted.

"This is strange," Colton began, "I've never known a car dealer that wasn't opened on Monday, ready and waiting at an early hour to make a sale. What does it say on that sign on the door?"

Eric couldn't read it from the patrol car, so he got out and walked up the few steps to the door. When he returned, he said, "Sorry, we're closed. Family emergency. Open tomorrow morning."

"No date? No time? No contact number?" Colton asked.

"Nope, nothing else. It seems someone really did leave in a hurry. There are usually at least two salespeople at these car lots. I wonder what happened to the other one?"

"Maybe they both belong to the same family, so they have the same emergency."

"Could be," Eric responded. "Either way, it looks like we have to wait until tomorrow to talk to the owner or manager or whoever might be here. I'll see if this place has a website. Maybe it gives a contact number."

They were quiet while Eric searched the web. There was a website, but it gave no further contact information than what was painted on this office door, which was the phone number for the place right here. Just to be sure, Eric tried the number. He stepped out of the car. He could hear the phone on the desk ringing in response to his call.

"That's not very modernized for this day and age. Most dealers would have their own iPhone or Smart Phone, or something like that, I would think, that this number would transfer to. If I owned a place like this, and it was my livelihood, I would be available to the public at any time. I would come after hours, if someone really wanted to buy a vehicle. Not on Sunday, of course."

"It just means another day of waiting. Let's go. I'm sure we can find plenty to do at the office, or, if we are lucky, we'll get a call about something."

They laughed.

There was simply nothing they could do about this. This was their next step and it could not be bypassed to go on to another step.

They didn't even know, right now, what the next step was.

Colton and Eric were at the car lot promptly at 7:30 on Tuesday morning. Although there had not been a date on the sign they had read on Saturday, they assumed it meant that an owner/manager/salesperson would be back this morning. State law in Arkansas prohibited auto sales on Sunday, so all car dealerships were closed.

That never made sense to Colton. Sunday was the one day of the week when most people were off work and could spend leisure time shopping for a vehicle. But, the law dated back to the old "Blue Laws," which were historically enacted by the courts to give the laborers a day of rest. It was actually religiously-based, but if a person were not a Christian, they could have their store open on Sunday, but they had to close another day of the week.

Auto dealerships in Arkansas were still held to this law.

They pulled in the car lot by way of the east entrance when another vehicle pulled in from the west entrance. They met in front of the sales office.

They all got out of the cars at the same time.

"Morning, gentlemen," the man began. "Beautiful day, isn't it?"

"I have to agree," Colton responded. "Are you the owner?"

"As a matter of a fact, I am," the man responded. "Bert King, at your service."

By this time Mr. King had unlocked the office door and they all went inside.

"If one of you is not here to buy a used car, I have to guess that this is an official visit. I can assure you I didn't do it."

The man laughed at his own joke. The two men grinned, although they both groaned inside. That was probably the oldest joke in the book.

"Let me get the coffee going and we can talk. I probably wouldn't make much sense without my first morning cup of joe, if you know what I mean. Didn't have any at home since I wanted to make sure I was here nice and early this morning. Have a seat, won't you?"

The man seemed at ease. It only took a few minutes to put the coffee in the drip machine, fill the pot and hit the start button. Mr. King walked to the door and removed the sign they saw Saturday afternoon, announcing the family emergency.

Colton nodded at the sign. "I hope it was nothing serious," he said.

"The father-in-law of my salesperson who was on duty Saturday afternoon had a heart attack. They took him to St. Mary's, up in Rogers, but he needed to be with his wife, of course. He's okay now. The father-in-law, I mean. Ordinarily, my other sales associate would also have been here, but she was sick that day. It all happens at the same time, doesn't it? I was far out-of-town, so I told Hayden to just put up a sign for this morning. I see he didn't leave a contact number or anything, just that we would be open now."

"Yeah, we came by late Saturday afternoon. We really do need to speak with you about something."

Just then they heard the crunch of tires on the gravel outside. A car came into view and parked.

"Customer," Mr. King said. He looked questioningly at both Colton and Eric.

"Go ahead, a few minutes won't make any difference."

Mr. King looked relieved. He would probably have to assure this customer that the sheriff was just here on unofficial business, so the man would not think anything funny was going on with the car sales.

King went out to greet the man, who obviously, by his gestures, wanted to look at a car on the far end of the lot. King walked with the man that way.

Colton and Eric looked at each other.

"Things seem to be conspiring against us with this case, for some reason. I know we are so close to solving this thing. As you say, I can feel it in my cells," Eric said.

It was about ten minutes before both men returned to the sales office. Colton and Eric stood.

"We'll just go outside while you conduct your business," Colton said. Both men touched their hats in acknowledgment to the other man and stepped outside. It took another fifteen minutes for the transaction to be completed.

"Hopefully, we won't scare any of his customers away. Maybe they will think we are here to arrest Mr. King for unscrupulous business practices, or something."

They watched as car after car passed by on Highway 62, most of them going east into Fayetteville. This was the equivalent of rush hour for the persons who lived west to be going into Fayetteville and other points east to work. There was about a three-mile stretch right here between the town of Farmington and Fayetteville. It was county jurisdiction. Colton thought how smart, business-wise, it had been for King to have a car lot right here. He avoided both city taxes, just having to pay Washington County taxes beyond the State and Federal.

He probably did a good business, normally, since he opened early and stayed open until 8:00 each evening most of the year, only closing at 6:00 during the winter, when it was dark by that time and the weather could be nasty.

They leaned on the patrol car. They started talking about the Sunday-closing law and how frustrated they had been when they arrived Saturday and found out the car lot was closed for the family emergency.

That lead them further into a funny discussion of some quirky Arkansas laws, most of them in the past now. There were laws that stated you couldn't keep an alligator in your bathtub and your dog couldn't bark after 6:00 p.m., or you would be fined. A female schoolteacher who bobbed her hair could not get a raise. And a man could beat his wife, but only once a month.

They laughed.

"What about the one that stated the Arkansas River couldn't rise above the bridge at Main St. in Little Rock? What were they going to do? Put the river in jail? That was so funny," Eric said.

"Those are all off the books, now, but I really like the one that's still on the books. It states that it is illegal to pronounce "Arkansas" incorrectly. I know there is a city in Kansas that is pronounced "Ar-kansas," like the state, but I really wonder where they got the "saw" on the end of Arkansas."

"The craziest thing to me," Colton added, "is the fact that Arkansas did not have a lottery until 2008. The good people of Arkansas kept voting it down every time it came up for a vote. I understand religious convictions and the teaching on gambling, and all that, and people vote with their religious consciences, I know, but look what was happening. The money goes for scholarships that allow a lot of students to attend colleges. The funds could have been available to students for years before that. People who want to play the lottery will find a way. They were going to the surrounding states to buy tickets and scratchers. The tax money was going to every state but Arkansas.

"The Oklahoma line is only thirty miles from here and if you live in the Dutch Mills area, Stilwell, Oklahoma is only about ten miles away. The same thing is true down the rest of the state and north across the line into Missouri. You know up at Siloam Springs from one side of a street to the next you are either in Arkansas or Oklahoma. At the line, all an Arkansas resident had to do was walk across to that Phillips 66 convenience store there to buy a lottery ticket or scratcher, or go across the other way to the casino."

"At least the money is being used in Arkansas now," Eric responded.

"Yeah, a good thing. But it could have been for many years before that."

He paused. "I wonder if you still get fined for spitting on the sidewalk?"

They laughed. They were still enjoying talking about all the weird laws when the men came out of the office, all smiles. They shook hands and the customer departed.

"Sorry about that," King apologized to the two men.

"That's fine, business is business, we understand that, but I really must insist that you give us some time now, regardless of who comes. Your first thought was correct, this is official police business."

Colton gave his best official tone.

Just then another car turned onto the lot. They looked at King.

"It's okay. It's my other salesperson, Carla. She can handle things now and we can talk. Just let me speak to her and we can go into my office."

They were settled there after King offered coffee and poured himself some, when they heard Carla come into the building.

"Now, what can I help you with?"

Colton knew he spoke innocently. There was nothing the man had done wrong and he knew it.

"We need to know who traded this vehicle in before August 10th." He handed a slip of paper to King with the vehicle type, a 2008 Toyota Corolla, Super White II, and the VIN.

"I almost remember that vehicle, but I don't know who brought it in or what they traded for. That week, I was up every day at the Rogers lot. I flipped through the paperwork for this place rather quickly at the end of that week. You do know I own lots in Springdale and Rogers also, don't you? I was there just as a morale booster. I try to visit each lot on a regular basis. They just don't know when I might show up. I figure that's the best way to make sure everything is going shipshape. Right?"

He grinned.

Colton did not have the impression that King would be a hard taskmaster, but you never could tell. The old thing saying about not being able to tell a book by its cover, like the assumptions they made about Van Hattabaugh, just might be true here. Many people had a public face and a private face.

Colton never surprised his staff with anything. He didn't think that was fair to them. Every once in a while, someone might have an off-day and not have the filing done, or a report on time, or something. It wasn't his job to make them feel intimidated about it. Things were taken care of.

"Let me see if Carla handled this," he said. He called to Carla, who came promptly to the door.

"Did you handle the trade-in of this vehicle before August 10th?" He handed her the slip of paper.

"Yes, I did, and I remember it because the woman, the wife, did not seem happy about having to trade it in. It had a noise, though, which only proved to be a bad alternator, which we replaced after the trade-in, of course. I recognized it right away. Also, we were not able to give her the price for the vehicle that she thought we should. She didn't know it had as many miles on it as it did. There are certain…categories…I guess you could call it, that if a vehicle has this number of miles on it, it has a certain value, or if it reaches the next category up in miles, it has a lesser value. Hers reached a certain point. She really argued about it, swearing that was not possible. But, odometers don't lie. For many years it has not been possible to turn back an odometer."

Colton knew that was not true. Generally speaking, yes, that's what the public thought, but it could be done by someone who knew how, but it took hours. He had even toyed with that idea on a case in Yellville, but nothing came of it. Car dealers like this had time, if they were so inclined. But, if they were caught it would mean their business and dealer's license, so it was usually not done.

"You didn't tell them that's all it was? The alternator?" Colton asked.

"Well, no…I…no," she said. She was nervous. She looked over at King.

The men knew what this meant, but this was not their purpose today. This meant when a customer came in because they did not recognize a noise their vehicle was making and thought it meant they needed another vehicle, these salespersons here, including King himself, they were sure, did not tell them it was something simple, that probably a few hundred dollars would cover, while the rest of the vehicle had no problems, and was worth keeping. After all, they were here to sell vehicles, not convince potential customers to keep what they had.

They looked at King and he knew they understood what had happened. Still, again, that was not their purpose this day. King didn't know that, though. What they did was not illegal, just morally questionable at times.

"We are only here to find out who traded in this vehicle, nothing else," Eric said.

Both King and Carla visibly relaxed but were not aware that was detected.

"Let me look at the paperwork for that day," Carla volunteered. "It will only take a few minutes."

The men watched as she went to a file cabinet in the outer office, behind her desk. She pulled out a fairly thick folder and started rummaging through it.

Business must have been good that day, Colton thought.

She found it, pulled it out from the others and came back to the office.

"Found it," she said. She handed it to King.

"Thanks, Carla," he said to her, nodding his head.

She knew that meant for her to leave, which she did, shutting the door behind her.

Yeah, more hard-nosed on his people than he wants people to think, Colton thought again. *If he has them 'trained' to obey his hand and head signals, that says a lot about this man.*

"Here it is," King said.

When he read the name to them, they both frowned. They shook their heads, not quickly remembering the couple.

They remembered the address, though, when King read that out to them.

Neither could hide the surprised expression on his face. Luckily, King was still looking down at the paperwork. He wondered if there was something else he should be telling the officers.

He looked up. "Anything else you need to know? It was a clean trade-in."

"What did they trade for?" Colton asked. *This should be interesting.*

"Let's see," King said. He flipped over a few more papers.

"Looks like a 2012 Ford Taurus, color Dark Blue Pearl Metallic. It didn't have anything wrong with it and they could afford it."

"Of course, it was a good car," Eric said, with a straight face. *He was sure it would have been a good car as they drove it off the lot.*

They stood up.

"Thank you, Mr. King, you have been most helpful."

They shook hands with the man and left.

King leaned back in his chair. *I wonder what that was all about? Just asking about a trade-in and then what car they bought? I wonder what they've done. The Sheriff doesn't waste his time, plus that of his chief deputy, for no reason.*

Just then another car pulled onto the lot. Carla was busy with another customer, so he stood up and met the man as he stepped out of his car.

It was going to be a good day. His last thought about the sheriff, though, as he walked toward his customer, was that he would keep eye on the paper, see if anything appeared there about the Taurus.

Chapter 38

They pulled out of the car lot heading west on Highway 62. They were just at the Farmington city limits. Let everyone going by slow down a little when they saw the patrol car. It wouldn't hurt them.

Colton was going to the home. He didn't want to waste any time.

"Pull up the information on that couple. Let's call them, see if we can see them today."

"She works during the day, but I got the impression that he didn't have a job."

"It won't do any good to talk to just one of them. See when she gets home. Tell the husband to call her, tell her to get home as soon as possible after work."

The IT tech at the department had set up a program that allowed an authorized person to access all the info they had gathered on all the homeowners and their vehicles during this part of the investigation. One thing was a phone number, or numbers, where they could always be contacted.

Eric did that on his smart phone.

"Looks like they gave us the landline number. Remember, the cell phone won't work at that place."

"Good. Call it. I bet you get the husband."

Eric did. He found out the wife should be home around 5:40 p.m. She had to come out of Fayetteville and it took that long. It would have been easy to talk to each of them separately, but Colton always wanted to watch the expressions on each face, eye contact, or whatever the couples might do between them. Sometimes, it was significant.

They arrived at the house around 5:30 p.m. They were greeted by the husband, who invited them inside to wait. They told him they would wait in the patrol car outside until the wife arrived home. After all, this was the couple who had owned the car with the matching dog hair inside.

That put them as close to the killer as they had ever been, which was never. If one of them was the killer, they didn't want to go into a situation they might not return from, and that could be the case if he realized they were that close to him.

Colton and Eric agreed that they were probably looking for a sociopath. Certainly one smart enough to commit a murder without leaving a trace. Or so he thought.

They got out of the car when they saw the wife's vehicle coming up the driveway. They had backed into the extra space on the property. The vehicle approaching was indeed the dark blue 2012 Ford Taurus this couple had bought from King Motors.

They asked if the husband would join them on the front porch. There were several chairs to sit in. They still did not want to go into the house.

"You really have our curiosity up, Sheriff, especially since you have talked with us before. Is this on the murder case?" The wife started the conversation.

"We need to ask both of you some further questions," Colton returned. He did not answer her question. "It's about the car you traded in to King Motors, the 2008 Toyota Corolla."

"Oh," the wife said. She was startled.

"That was the last thing I expected you to ask about. I really hated giving that car up, but it started making a noise. My husband here," she gestured toward the man, "said that it sounded like something serious, that we really should get another vehicle, so that's why we went there. We knew we couldn't afford a new vehicle. We had heard some good things about King Motors."

Yeah, like not telling them the noise they heard was only the alternator. This man must not know anything about vehicles, Colton thought.

"How long had you owned the Corolla?" he asked. Eric was talking notes.

"Oh, several years," she responded. "It got good gas mileage, which was one of the reasons I like it. This Taurus certainly doesn't get as good as it. I travel to the University and back every day, that's around seventy miles every day. I'm really disappointed in this Ford."

Now Colton remembered that this woman was one of the chatterboxes of Dutch Mills.

"Do you attend the church there at Dutch Mills?"

"No, we don't. We are not Baptists, but have a different belief. We go to a little church outside of Stilwell, this way on the highway. It's a non-denominational church, so we agree with its teachings."

The wife was still answering.

"Do you go to Dutch Mills often?"

"I thought we were in Dutch Mills. That's what everyone calls where we live here, anyway. I really don't think of it as Dutch Mills, simply that we live out in the country between Dutch Mills and Stilwell, maybe sometimes we say Evansville, but nobody seems to know where that is. More people seem familiar with where Stilwell is, so that's why we say that. My mother used to live here before she died, she lived here for almost forty years, and she always referred to where she lived as Dutch Mills."

Yep, one of the chatterboxes. Way more info that any-one needs. Well, maybe not in this case. Maybe the more she talks, she will let something slip, Colton thought.

"I meant the little community of Dutch Mills, itself," he said.

"Oh, of course you did. Sorry. Well, no, we never turn into that community. Since we don't go to church there, and we really don't have any friends there, then we don't really have a reason to go there, now, do we? It would be pretty crazy of us to go through there and down State Line Road to get here, don't you think?"

"We are just asking some general questions. We are going to several homes again that we went to before. Just routine. Back to the car. You told us at the time that you take your little dog to the vet sometimes. Did you take him in the Corolla?"

"Yes, of course. He was pretty sick about three months ago, during the summer. We let him out to do his business. We went back in the house but after a while we remembered him. We called but he didn't come. We out to look for him. We found him out in the woods, and he tried to get up to come to us, but he couldn't. He finally did, but was very wobbly. Wayne picked him up and brought him back to the house, but he didn't get better in a day or two. So, we had to take him to the vet. The vet said probably he had been bit by some poisonous spider or something in the woods. Didn't look like a snake bite, or there would have been marks and he would have been swollen. The vet looked him over good, but didn't see any bites. Poor doggy! He got better, though, and now we watch him, don't let him go into the woods. He's pretty much trained now to go potty nearer the house."

Colton pictured that in his mind as one whole para-graph, maybe even one whole sentence. The woman hadn't take a breath during the whole spiel.

The forensics tech said she had found another dog hair in the Corolla, plus the matching hair from the murdered dog, so it must be from that dog. Made sense.

"No other dog has been in the Corolla, at least not since you owned it?"

"No, not that I know of. I said we owned the car for several years, but we bought it new, in 2008. But, that's several years, I guess, isn't it?" She smiled.

Not only a chatterbox, but a dingbat, Colton thought. She could have said that in the first place.

"Of course it is, Baby," answered the man, patiently. He looked at the officers. They understood he knew what he was dealing with in this woman. He must have the patience of Job.

"Did you ever let anyone use, drive, or borrow the Corolla?" Colton asked. He almost held his breath the whole time they were talking to these two. He certainly didn't want them to think they were being interrogated, just having a chat.

"No, I've always been very firm about that. It was a new car and I didn't want anyone else wrecking it or something, not even a fender bender. A car is never the same after that. Well, that is, I sure didn't ever let anyone else borrow it. You didn't, did you, Wayne, all those times you took me to work when the weather was bad. You didn't let anyone use it, did you, surely not in bad weather?"

"No, I never did, I knew how you felt about that car," he answered.

"Well, it just cost so much and I had to work so hard all the time to make the payment, I just didn't feel like having anyone else drive it."

"I know, I know, don't get excited." Wayne patted her arm and she seemed to quiet down a little.

This was getting nowhere fast. Colton decided to ask questions in another way. The forensics didn't lie. The

Corolla had been the car with the matching dog hair. It was just a matter of tracking down who put it there!

"You told us last time you owned a shotgun. Do you have any other guns around the place?"

It was Wayne's turn to answer.

"No, we don't. I keep the shotgun around to go hunting with friends from time to time. As a matter of fact, my friend and I were planning to go this weekend. It's the season for dove and squirrel. We'll probably try for a deer when the season opens. My friend has an extra rifle I use then."

"And no other, rifles, pistols, or anything like that?"

Colton just felt there had to be something here. There was something he was missing. It had to be his fault. Maybe he was just not asking the right questions. These two sure weren't going to supply the answers without direct questions.

The man and woman looked at each other. They started to shake their heads, but the woman spoke.

"Well, we should have had another one," began the woman.

"What do you mean?" Colton asked. Maybe this was the break they needed.

"Well, my mom had a pistol around here for years and years. In fact, my dad had it for years before he left and left it for my mom, so she would have it for protection. When he left, you know, that put mom here all by herself, way out here in the country, with no one around. I don't even think if you yelled real loud that a neighbor could hear you. Well, maybe if everything around was very still and quiet, you know, no cars going by on the highway, that person not listening to the radio or TV or anything. The conditions would have to be just right, though, for anyone to hear, not even the couple across the highway.

"So, your dad left it with her," Colton urged, but he didn't want to appear too eager for the answer.

"And what did she do with it?" Colton asked.

"Well, nothing. She just kept it by her bed all the time. Even during the daytime she left it there. Even the grandkids knew not to go into her bedroom, that the pistol was there." She paused.

"When she passed away, she didn't leave it here?"

Colton had the crazy thought that she sure didn't take it with her!

"Of course, she did, and it should have been ours after that. After all, we moved in with her to take care of her during her old age and we were here for a year before she passed away. That pistol should have been ours. Wayne really wanted it, too."

"What kind of pistol was it?"

She looked toward Wayne.

"It was a .22-caliber long barrel, but it was an older one. Like she said," he nodded toward his wife, "her mom had it for many years and they both had it the whole forty years she lived here. It might have been older than that. It was one of those that didn't have a safety on it. I wanted it because of that. Someone who wasn't aware that it wasn't made with a safety, but thought a safety might be on, might pick it up and accidently make it go off."

"She kept bullets in it?"

"Of course she did, it was for protection," the woman answered "What good is an empty gun if you need or use it for protection? What are you going to say to a robber that breaks into your home, oh, excuse me while I load this gun so I can shoot you?"

"She used it so rarely that it probably had the same bullets in it that my dad had made. He made about a dozen for it, then decided it wasn't worth all the time and effort. He had a loader, but the tornado took that away when it took the garage and everything in it."

Wayne pointed to a spot near the house.

"A detached garage sat there. The tornado took the garage, left the car sitting, then put two huge trees that grew by the garage down on the car. Obviously, in that order. Tornadoes are funny things."

Colton certainly didn't want to get off track talking about tornadoes. This woman could probably talk the rest of the evening about them.

Wayne was continuing, "…but her dad said that was okay, that Walmart had the same caliber, so a store-bought bullet was okay. Just thought he would try his hand at making them, that was all."

Colton's thoughts were racing.

The dog hair.

The older, .22-caliber pistol.

Homemade bullets.

Colton just knew he was looking at the murder weapon. He just had to find out where it was.

"And why don't you have it now?" he asked.

"Because her sister took it, that's why. I can't prove that, because she told us it must have been someone after the mom's death, because there were so many people coming and going until the funeral, and even after that. A person would have to go down the hall next to the mom's bedroom to go to the bathroom, and the pistol was right in plain sight, right inside the bedroom door, on the nightstand. So, technically, I guess it could have been anyone. But I don't believe her. I think she took it. The wife and I argue about it all the time. She doesn't think her sister would lie about something like that."

"Would she still have it, if she had taken it, do you think?"

"I suppose she would," the woman said. "I can't think of any reason why she wouldn't have it, since she wanted it to remember mom by. I could ask her, if you like."

"Oh, no, don't do that," Colton responded. "It doesn't matter, anyway."

He certainly didn't want her calling the sister.

He knew the sister had the gun.

Just a feeling.

"We need to go. If we think of anything else, we will come again. If you think of anything, anything unusual or different about the car or gun, please call us. Thank you for your time."

Chapter 39

I t was dark.
The couple went down the steps and walked out to the car with them, telling them if there was anything else they needed, please call.

Eric walked around to the passenger side of the patrol car and Colton was reaching for the handle, when the woman spoke.

"Oh, wait, there is something," she began.

In unison, the two men turned and stared at the woman.

"Well, you just said anything unusual, and maybe this is not that unusual, or out of the ordinary or anything like that, but you also asked if anyone else had driven the Corolla."

"Yes?" Colton asked. He was beginning to feel excited. He knew Eric was, too, since they both usually had some of the same feelings.

"Well, my sister did once. Well, I don't know if you could really call it driving it, not in the real sense, I mean, she didn't take a trip in it, or anything like that. She only drove it to go after doughnuts for us once when I stayed with her. Just visiting, I was, nothing serious happening. I was asleep and she got up early, so she went. She even went out in the pouring rain, but she said we didn't see each other that often, so she wanted me to have my favorite. Doughnuts, that is. She's a good sister," the woman finished.

She had a big smile on her face, remembering the occasion.

"And when was this?" Colton asked.

"That's funny," the woman said. "It would have been the morning of the murder. But she doesn't live in Dutch Mills. She lives up in Siloam."

"And why were you there?" Colton asked. He was more certain than ever that they were closing in on the killer.

"She invited me to come for the weekend. She said we didn't get together often enough. So, I went straight from work to her house that Thursday evening. We had a great dinner, then hot chocolate before bedtime. I slept very late the next morning. I felt great. I must have been more stressed and tired from work than I thought. The visit was just what the doctor ordered, so to speak. I hadn't really gone to a doctor, of course. I stayed until Saturday afternoon. I don't like to drive after dark and don't like to miss church, so I came home then. But I had a great time with my Sis."

Colton had thought of something.

"Does your sister own a car?"

"Of course she does," she answered.

Why, Colton thought, *is everything from this woman like pulling teeth?*

"What kind of car is it?"

Diane told him what she thought it was, and he remembered it. Her description was close enough.

"Why didn't she drive her own car to go after doughnuts? Why drive the Corolla?"

"Why, she had a flat. I saw it. And she was so nice. She had my car door open with a fan on it, so I wouldn't get my bottom damp when I had to drive home! She even unscrewed the overhead light so it wouldn't run down my battery. Now, who would have thought of that?"

A killer? Colton thought. *trying to cover up something? After she had used this car?*

This was probably the best at self-control he had ever experienced. Erin was quiet, not a sound from him.

"Does that help?"

"Thank you again for everything," Colton said.

He motioned for Eric to go to the car. As the couple turned away, they heard her say to the husband, "…and be sure to take that trash down to the barrel."

Something clicked in Colton's brain.

Trash! Of course, the trash, he thought.

"Wait," he called to the couple. They stopped halfway up the steps and turned toward him. He had noticed the big trash barrel down at the end of the driveway, over to the side of the highway at the culvert when they turned in the driveway.

"When does the trash get picked up here?"

"The truck comes by early Fridays, every other week. Why is that important?" asked Wayne.

Colton just waved it off.

"Nothing. Just a thought," he said. "Thanks, again."

Chapter 40

They did not speak until they had gone the three-quarters of a mile on South Arkansas 244 to Highway 59. They turned left (you can't go straight) toward Fayetteville.

Colton broke the silence. His hands were shaking on the steering wheel.

"You realize what this means, don't you?" he asked Eric.

Eric frowned. He really had not put anything together about what they had just heard. He must have forgotten previous conversations with all the other homeowners they had interviews. But Colton hadn't forgotten any of them.

Especially now.

Every conversation was coming back to him.

"What?" Eric asked. "That woman was sure a Chatty Cathy, wasn't she? My sister had one of those dolls when she was a child, and this woman reminded me of that doll."

"You really don't see it?" Colton asked.

"No, I guess not. What are you seeing?"

"We just found our killer, that's what I'm seeing. It's as plain as the nose on your face. It all fits together so perfectly. I know we can even prove it," Colton answered.

He explained it all to Eric, putting the pieces together. Eric was astonished. He had not seen, but he had not remembered everything that Colton did. He had to agree.

"Everything certainly makes perfect sense the way you explain it, but we do have to prove it in black and white."

"But we can, we can!" Colton almost shouted. His voice was certainly several octaves higher than it usually was. "But we can't say anything about it, yet, not even to the wives, okay? We have to have all our ducks in a row with this. As I said about that dog hair, I don't want a young, I-think-I'm-smarter-than-you lawyer getting this person off on a technicality, or something. Every comma, every "i" and every "t" is going to be just right on this. No mistakes, no typos, no nothing! The killer is not going to know what hit her.

"Tomorrow we go to the county prosecutor for an arrest warrant. We have to get the Siloam Springs Police Department to come with us. It's their jurisdiction."

Colton started singing "*Tomorrow*," from the musical "*Annie.*"

Eric couldn't help but catch Colton's mood.

He sang along.

Eric had doubts, though. Everything seemed so circumstantial.

Chapter 41

arsha knew something had happened. She guessed it had something to do with the murder investigation.

"I'm not even going to ask," she said that evening.

"Thanks. I just can't say anything right now, you know that. I want to call Clark, though. He'll want to know about this."

It didn't offend her that he went to his office and shut the door. She would know about it soon enough.

Clark answered after the first ring.

"We did it, we did it!" Colton whispered. He didn't think Marsha ever tried to listen in on his official calls, but he really didn't want anyone to know about this too soon.

"Colton, you can't fool me, I'd know that voice anywhere. What did you do?"

"We know who the killer is."

"In that Dutch Mills case? Really? How so?" Clark was all ears. The last time they had talked, there were still no clues.

"Well, I don't want to sound like I know everything, not even…"

Clark interrupted him. "Don't tell me. Your 'hair-brained' theory worked? If that's what you're getting ready to tell me, I can't believe it. Now, don't get me wrong here, I know how great you are, your feelings and how intuitive you are, but I never thought that idea would work. I thought you were wasting your time. Tell me all about it."

"Let me start from the beginning with the clues and facts and how I put them together. I even made a list for you. Can you go to your computer? I'll attach it and send it, you can print it out, and we can look at it together.

"Oh, I'm sorry," Colton continued. "I didn't even ask how you and Betty were, if you had time to listen to this, or anything. I guess I'm just so excited I thought everyone would be able to listen to me."

"We're fine, and, yes, I have time to listen, especially to this. I wouldn't miss it for the world. Just give me a few minutes to get to the computer and pull up everything."

They still had a PC. They also had a laptop, but Betty liked to work on the PC. Even though she had a smart phone, she said her computer didn't need to move around. Clark wanted to be able to pull the list up on a full-size monitor. In a few minutes, he had the information before him.

"Wow, what a list. Start, and I'll follow you," he told Colton.

Clark had to print out three pages.

"This is based on my "hair-brained theory" which is what the men call it. I just had the idea that the killer must have left some clue, or even left the house *with* even one clue, and why not a dog hair? The dog would have jumped off the bed, ran into the dining room, and it is one of those breeds that really shed. Hairs probably flew everywhere off the dog in its agitated state. Perhaps the killer had picked one up on his clothes somehow, it got in a cuff, or in a pocket, wherever, when the killer was wiping the floor to conceal his tracks. Perhaps the killer even brushed up against the dog. I thought perhaps the wind/rain had not blown/washed the hair(s) away and it fell off in the vehicle. We had only one man's word that the vehicle *could have been* a "small, whitish" one."

"Column on left gives detail(s), column on right gives further info on column one, with dates. These are not necessarily in this order; they can be arranged correctly later. But this is close enough for government work. Ha!"

"Small, whitish" vehicle seen near crime scene at time of murder by Henry Carlton	Only Carlton man saw this. (June 4th)
All homeowners questioned and vehicles vacuumed for dog hairs/all debris	Done (June 8th – October 17th)
Lab tech found matching dog hair to hair of slain dog in vehicle	Dog hair found in 2008 Toyota Corolla, a special white color (October 20th). Could be "small, whitish" car described by Carlton, bottom of hill from crime scene
2008 Toyota traced to Van Hattabaugh	Van Hattabaugh bought Corolla from King Motors, Farmington (August 11th)
Corolla had been traded in to King Motors by Diane and Wayne Watson, South Arkansas Highway 244, Dutch Mills	(August 7th)

Diane Watson at first said no one had driven the Corolla, then remembered that her sister had used it, just once, to go buy doughnuts/ pastries during severe rainstorm while Diane was staying overnight with sister	(who goes out in a storm like this just for doughnuts?) (June 4th)
Sister put fan on interior of vehicle to dry it because it got rain in it going in/out for the doughnuts. Disconnected overhead light, supposedly not to run the battery down.	How much rain really gets inside a vehicle just getting in/out of a vehicle once? (June 4th) Could the overhead light have still been disconnected because she did it so it would not give out any light at the end of the road/bottom of hill, Dutch Mills?
Sister's vehicle had flat tire when she wanted to go for the doughnuts, that's why she used the Corolla.	Accidentally? On purpose? A coincidence only?
Diane Watson complained at the time of trade-in of Corolla to King Motors that the car somehow had too much mileage on it, she didn't remember	Was there too much mileage on the car because the sister drove to Dutch Mills the morning of June 4th , killed the pastor's wife, and returned to Siloam Springs, all before Diane woke up?

that number as the mileage, so it put the car at a lesser trade-in value.	
Diane slept a long time, didn't get up until around 11:00 a.m. Was surprised she slept so long.	Drugged? Sister put substance in hot chocolate to make Diane sleep soundly and for a long time? Sister made hot chocolate for both of them that night before going to bed. Sister's was normal?
Trash pickup out in the country, at Diane's place, is early every other Friday morning. Sister would have known time of trash pickup because their mom lived there for forty years.	Was this an alternate Friday pickup time? WHERE DOES TRASH GO FROM THERE? Could killer have put clothes worn at crime scene/weapon in trash bag and it was picked up as trash, as usual?
Diane admitted their mom had a .22-caliber pistol for many years for protection, they suspect sister took it after mom's death. Father (years ago) had made some handmade bullets for it, but tornado took the apparatus away.	Murder weapon was an older type .22-caliber pistol, slug was handmade. (Apparatus for making handmade bullets would have been proof) But still murder slug was handmade.

> Betting that the killer could not stand to get rid of the pistol in remembrance of her mother.

"Have you had time to read that yet?"

"Yes, I just finished, and, wow, you really have some evidence there. But are you sure it's not all just circumstantial? Do you have the gun, or know where to find it when you go with your warrant to arrest this killer?" Clark was concerned.

"No, I don't know where the gun actually is, but I would bet a year's salary that it is still with the killer. It's a reminder of the mother. Why would someone get rid of it? The killer probably thinks she has it hidden so well that nobody will ever find it."

"That's just a supposition on your part. It just might be at the bottom of Lake Tenkiller over in Oklahoma. Or at the bottom of Beaver Lake there in Northwest Arkansas. Colton, I know all this looks good, but just what exactly can you prove from this? Really, truly prove?"

"Now, Clark, don't go raining on my parade," Colton said. He really didn't want to start doubting himself over this whole thing.

"Well, a hurricane rained on your evidence that night. I just don't see how you can make a murder conviction out of this. Does this woman still go to church in Dutch Mills? Did she even know the pastor's wife?"

"She used to go to church there, so she knew the pastor's wife then. She's lived the last two years in Siloam Springs, in Benton County, over on the Oklahoma line. It's about twenty-five miles north of Dutch Mills."

"So, are you just going to go ask her if she killed the pastor's wife at Dutch Mills? You know sociopaths, and psychopaths, for that matter. They can look you straight in the face and lie, none of those micro-expressions on her face, that you are so big into, no 'tell' to give herself away. They can pass a lie detector test, also.

"She would have no sense of right or wrong, or understand another's feelings, much less care about the dog. If she's a psychopath, she will lie to you because she doesn't have a conscience. She will act like everyone else so she can 'hide in plain sight.' Look at all the major serial killers. Neighbors were all totally surprised when he or she was arrested for whatever number of murders and or tortures they had committed. They just seemed like ordinary folks, sometimes even babysitting the kids, which I'm sure made the parents sick when an arrest was made.

"If she's a psychopath she will have a weak conscience. That might be where you will get her, although she would probably be a cold, calculating killer. If she can kill, she certainly can lie like a pro. She may never do it again.

"The really important thing that worries me is the fact that you don't have the murder weapon. How are you going to justify that?"

"I am going to search her place high and low. If she has carpet, it's coming up and I'll check the flooring under that. I will make sure there are no hidden panels anywhere. If I have to tear up the place to satisfy myself whether the gun is there or not, I will. I think I have enough in the budget to fix it back, but if I don't, I'll pay for it myself. I just know it's there."

Colton sounded so sure that Clark was almost willing to believe that he *would* find the gun.

"You can only do what you know to do. Or, is this a case of feeling it in your cells, as you are fond of saying?"

"I can feel it in my cells," Colton answered. "I don't think I've ever been so sure of anything in my whole career."

"Then go for it," Clark encouraged Colton. "You know I'll be thinking about you and hoping all goes your way. You need it, no, you deserve it. You deserve to be able to solve this."

"Thanks for your vote of confidence," Colton answered, sincerely. He knew his friend really did wish him success.

They talked a few more minutes and hung up.

Chapter 42

Eric met Colton at the office and they went together to the county prosecutor's office. This office was located in the County Courthouse, which was in Downtown Fayetteville. They would not be going to the original courthouse, which was built in 1905 and was an architectural wonder, now on the National Register of Historic Places. The new courthouse was located on the corner, just north of the original building. The original building contained records and just a few offices.

They hit a snag when they arrived at the prosecutor's office. His assistant told them that he would not be in this day and half of the next day. It was some personal business he had to take care of. It had been on the calendar for a while.

"Kevin, do you know exactly when Joshua will return? We have some very, very important business to discuss with him?"

They all knew each other and worked closely with each other on country business.

Kevin heard the urgency in Colton's voice. He sensed how important it was.

"Just tomorrow at 1:00, just after lunch. He did not leave an emergency number. You know how he is about being disturbed on his personal time. I really hesitate to call him, about anything," he added.

Colton just shrugged.

"It is very important, but it has waited until now, so I suppose it can wait another day. But it is important enough, that if you have anyone in his 1:00 slot tomorrow, please change it or cancel it or do whatever you need to do to get us there first. We'll be here at 12:45 waiting for him."

He looked at him questioningly, but he was not about to tell him what it was.

"Okay, will do, Sheriff, you know you will always have top priority."

"Thanks, Kevin, and don't worry, you will know soon enough what it's all about."

"I don't doubt that," he smiled at the two men.

One thing, though, he did not have the Dutch Mills murder case on his mind, so he would never have guessed that. No one but the department knew how hard they all had worked on this, or about the pairing of teams to follow the "hair trail," which was one of the names the men had given it.

Nor, when the arrest was made, would they guess the time involved, even then. The general public would just assume it had been another day at the office, was just the job of the sheriff and he did it.

The pressure they had continued to face would never be felt by anyone as much as by Colton and Eric, and the most by Colton.

Chapter 43

They said nothing more until they were outside on the sidewalk.

"It's early but are you hungry?" Colton asked Eric. "Well, I guess I could go for a bagel and some coffee," Eric agreed.

"If I remember correctly, The Old Post Office Café on the Square will probably have something available. Maybe we can talk him into fixing us something, anyway."

"Yeah, probably. Let's just walk. We always have a reserved spot here at the courthouse. No use trying to find one just a few blocks closer to the Square."

"Beautiful morning for it, anyway," Colton agreed.

This was a café that had been remodeled in the basement of the old county courthouse on the square. It kept the old ambience, with the original ceiling and hardwood throughout. It also had a display of old post office boxes, about a hundred, on one wall, which were from the original post office. It stayed full, especially at lunchtime, with employees from shops and offices around the square. It advertised a 10-minute delivery of certain lunches on the menu, so everyone could have lunch and get back to work within an hour. At this time of day, there would be plenty of room.

They were both avoiding the subject on their minds, they knew that. They were too frustrated to talk about it. In about a half block, Colton brought it up.

"Damn! It seems like everything in the world is *still* conspiring against us in this case. First, we had to go back the next day to King Motors, then wait a whole day for the woman there on Highway 244 to come home from work, now this. Waiting for Joshua!

It's just been hurry up and wait at every turn."

Eric didn't say it, but he wondered if perhaps something, someone, or whatever you wanted to call it, somewhere was telling them not to do what they were beginning to do. If nothing came of this, and it all depended on finding that damned gun, then poor Colton would look like a bigger fool than ever. He would never live down his "hairbrained theory" and really have to eat crow.

Instead, Eric said, "Well! You really are a tortoise, aren't you, Colton? You have just slowly, but steadily, kept after that dog hair theory. And to have it in a bag that we collected, that's something."

Never would Colton know that he had any doubts about Colton's theory.

"You collected, you mean," Colton responded. "I'm sure it's thanks to your meticulous vacuum job, on each and every vehicle, that the hair was in the bag. It could have been so easy to miss it, maybe in those tiny spaces between the seats and console that you can't even get your fingers down if something falls there. How did you vacuum in those spaces, by the way?"

"I used that tiny brush to bring anything down that might be stuck there. Then, I went at them from the underneath side, from the back floorboard. Just seemed the best thing to do. Besides, I've vacuumed my own vehicles enough times to know how to do it. Mary gave me that assignment years ago. I get to wash and vacuum the car and SUV."

"Good, sensible Eric. You've been a godsend to me on this force, you know that, don't you? I know I haven't told you that often enough. I mean it. I really do appreciate your dedication. Mainly, I appreciate how you and the other guys, and woman, of course, have accepted me here in Washington County."

"Thank you, Chief, and you're an acceptable type of person," Eric responded.

They laughed. They had reached the Grill by then.

Chapter 44

I wonder if this is right," Colton said.

"Uumm…" Marsha groaned. She had just drifted off to sleep.

"I said, I wonder if this is right," Colton repeated.

Still half asleep, Marsha said, "Is what right?"

"The fact that we are asking the country prosecutor for an arrest warrant for this woman. What if I'm wrong?"

By this time, Marsha had turned from her side to her back.

"You have doubts? You?" she asked, as she turned to her other side, facing Colton, who was on his back. "I don't think I've ever known you to have doubts. Is this about the Dutch Mills murder?"

"Yes, and what if I'm wrong?" he repeated.

"You've never told me all the facts, not fully, just bits and pieces. Why don't you tell me? You're certainly not going to get this off your mind, this doubt, which means neither of us is going to get any sleep tonight. So, what's your main doubt? What do you have as evidence? Enough for an arrest?"

He proceeded to go through the facts, in a laundry list, sort of like the list he gave to both Clark and Eric. With Marsha, though, he could throw in more personal comments and opinions. He knew it wouldn't go any further than this bedroom.

Marsha absorbed all the facts.

"Wow!" she said. "Are you sure you haven't made all this up? Is this going to be your first 'whodunit' or something? They say truth is stranger than fiction, but this string of facts is really something.

"But…" she paused. "The way I see it, you need to find the gun. You can think all you want to, and the evidence can point to the gun, but without it, it's still circumstantial, in my opinion. Do you have any idea where it could be?"

"Roy thought perhaps the killer might have thrown it down a crevice along that ridge on the Arkansas/Oklahoma line, he says there are lots of them, because he goes hunting out that way. My first thought was that it is probably in a landfill somewhere, about one hundred feet below a bunch of garbage. After all, this woman has had four months to dispose of it. Surely, she could think of a good place where it would never be found. I mean, even I could think of somewhere in that length of time.

"Then, there's a feeling I have…"

"I knew it," Marsha laughed. "You always have feelings and they have always proved true. That's why I wonder why you doubt just now that you are doing the right thing. But, okay, what is your feeling right now?"

"The sister said the pistol had belonged to their mom, who had lived in the same spot there in Dutch Mills for forty years, that the dad left, but gave the gun to the mother for protection. The mom kept it by her bed all those years.

"I'm betting the woman is so sentimental, at least about her mother, that she decided to keep the gun in her memory. The woman looked at this pistol on the bedside table all these years, she probably sees her mother in it."

"Do sociopaths, psychopaths, do that? Do they have sentimental thoughts and feelings like that? I thought there was no conscience there, with them, I mean, and you seem to think this woman must be a sociopath.

"And what about motive? She hasn't lived in Dutch Mills for over two years. Did she even know the pastor's wife that well? Did she have anything against her? Have any run-ins with her, that sort of thing?"

"No one has said anything like that about her. In fact, the ones with the problems were the neighbor's son I told you about and the church organist."

"Do you have to prove motive here to make an arrest or establish guilt?" she asked. "I would think that, in any case, anywhere, because I've never understood why a court of law has to establish motive, that if it can be proved that a person killed someone, that is the fact. Period. Who really cares what a person's motive is?"

"No, I can't think of a motive for this woman, not right now, but you're right. I've always thought that, also. If a person did it, he or she did it. Who cares why? But this no motive business does play into all the circumstantial evidence."

Nothing was said for a few minutes. They were both wide-awake now with no hope of getting any sleep this night.

"But I need to do this, this arrest. Then, as I told Clark and Eric, I will search everywhere for that gun."

"I know you will, and I know you will find it, this because of your feelings. As I said, I've never known them to be wrong. Now, why not lie back and relax, both your body and mind. Try to get some sleep. You have a big day tomorrow."

They settled back in the bed. Marsha hoped Colton would sleep.

Just then, he spoke again.

"I almost made a mistake here, you know, I didn't say this when I was telling you, but I decided on Friday before I left the office, and told Eric, that this Monday I was going to arrest Ricky Carlton for the murder. All that vehicle evidence, which would be all circumstantial, too, in the end, although you know I don't believe in circumstances, pointed to him.

"Marsha, I almost ruined a young man's life by arresting him and putting something like this on his record. Right now, he doesn't have a record, then he would have a felony arrest. How could I have come so close to doing that?"

Marsha was quiet for a moment.

"If that's true, then all this may not be circumstantial," she said, quietly.

It was Colton's turn to look over at her.

"What do you mean?" he asked.

"Well, maybe there are forces in play here beyond you and even beyond your feelings. You said the young forensics lab tech found the dog hair from the Corolla on Saturday, one day after you had made up your mind to get a warrant for young Carlton's arrest. Instead of that, finding the dog hair put you on tracking down the vehicles, from one to the other, the owner, where the car had been, who had borrowed or driven it. I don't think it was an accident that the one woman in Dutch Mills just 'happened' to mention that she had been at her sister's and the sister used the car. You had mentioned that this same woman was surprised at the mileage on that vehicle, thinking it should not have been that much. It just put them up into a lesser trade-in value.

"I think that all these seemingly little incidental facts that were mentioned at one time or another, but just in time to prevent you from arresting the wrong person, were not just thrown out into the universe for no reason. Call it Fate, kismet, God, 'The Force,' or whatever you like, I don't think all this is circumstantial.

"You're doing the right thing, Colton, just go with the instincts you have. You'll find that gun. I know it."

He reached over and took her hand.

"What would I do without you?" he asked. "You just reinforced my feelings."

"We both know, also," she continued, "that even if you are wrong and never find that gun, you would never forgive yourself for not trying, going for it."

"You're right, of course," he responded. "I think I've just let all my thoughts of failure about that case in Yellville get the better of me."

"You mean the Ellison case?" she asked. "But you did arrest someone for that murder. It was not your fault that the judge declared a mistrial and then the county prosecutor there decided not to bring it to trial again. Both of these actions were beyond your control, you just had to deal with the outcomes. Who knows what the decision of a jury would have been there? But you certainly did your duty. This case is not like that at all.

"Now, please go to sleep," she concluded.

"Yes, ma'am," he replied.

He smiled in the darkness as he listened to Marsha settling.

His rock.

Chapter 45

At 12:45 the next day they were waiting for Joshua to make it to the office. He saw them the minute he came through the door. He raised his eyebrows. "What's up, guys?" He turned to his assistant.

"Looks like you need to hold all calls, anything. Don't disturb us, okay?"

He agreed.

For these two, the sheriff and chief deputy, to be waiting for him, this had to be something important. He was sharp enough to wonder if it had something to do with the Dutch Mills murder. He hadn't heard of any other cases that important to the county at this particular time.

He was not wrong, as he soon found out. That briefcase that Colton had, contained paperwork from the car dealer, the DMV, all papers of the two vehicle transactions.

Colton presented the facts as they had them. He gave Joshua a copy of the list he had sent Clark and Eric.

Unfortunately, Joshua also saw everything as circumstantial. It took Colton and Eric over two hours to explain everything from their point of view.

Joshua leaned back in his chair, one hand on an arm, his elbow in the air.

Colton and Eric didn't say a word. They knew he was processing all he had heard, thinking about it.

Joshua thought about Colton from their university and frat days here at the University of Arkansas. Colton was then, as now, an honest man of integrity, with excellent character, possessing a decent quality few men had in his position with all its temptations.

Joshua remembered a time when he was in the den of the frat house when four guys went up to Colton and asked him if he were interested in having a copy of the final test of one of the professors, a hard-nosed teacher. There seemed to be an opportunity to obtain said test. He plainly remembered Colton's response, "No, thanks, guys, if I can't make it on my own, I just won't." The other guys had shrugged and walked away. Colton's head went back down to the books in front of him on the desk.

Another time they found themselves alone in the den. They talked and shared future ambitions. Colton wanted to be a county sheriff and Joshua wanted to be a county prosecutor, especially here, in Washington County, his home county. It wasn't lack of ambition on the part of either, just what they thought would be the ideal positions.

"You're not Captain of the Arkansas State Troopers, you're just the county sheriff," Joshua said to Colton, with a grin.

"And you're not Arkansas State's Attorney General, just Washington County prosecutor. What's wrong with you?"

Eric's eyes flew open and he looked from one to the other.

They laughed. They both knew they referred to that particular conversation. The "just" was part of the joke between them.

"Happy?" Colton asked Joshua.

"We are, totally," came the reply. Colton knew Joshua meant his wife, who held a prominent position at the University, and his two children. His son would graduate from the University this year and his daughter was a freshman. Same frat, same sorority as the parents.

"You?" Joshua asked of Colton.

"Couldn't be better," Colton replied. "It just took me a little longer than you to get here."

Eric relaxed. He would ask Colton about this exchange later.

Colton was happy when he first came to this county to hear that Joshua was county prosecutor. Joshua clapped loudest for Colton at the reception. He had been the first to congratulate him.

Several times over the past two years these two had come before him, asking for arrest warrants. Once, for sure, Colton had presented even less evidence, but he had made it stick, and the man was convicted.

Joshua never doubted Colton on any of those other occasions, so why was he doubting now?

Suddenly, he knew he didn't.

He leaned forward and called the judge. He briefly explained what was needed. He listened for a few more minutes, then hung up.

"Gentlemen, your warrant will be waiting when you get there. Better hurry!"

They laughed as they stood up.

The judge's chambers were one floor up in this building.

The men shook hands. Joshua wished them luck, but he knew it would be more than that.

He knew the excellent job Colton did right now as county sheriff. If he were to believe anyone, it would be Colton. They met now socially, occasionally. If Colton thought this was the way to go, then Joshua would support him.

Joshua's next appointment was waiting, had been for a while. But, if something was important, it was worth waiting for.

Colton and Eric walked out of the judge's office around 4:00 p.m. It was just in time to get in the pre-rush hour traffic going north toward Springdale and other points north. There seemed to be an unusual amount of traffic on Interstate 71, but Colton figured that was only because of their excitement. The traffic here was always heavy.

They called the Chief of the Siloam Springs Police Department to see if he would meet them.

Chapter 46

As was her habit, she fixed herself a sliced ham sandwich, with a slice of real cheese, none of that processed junk for her, and mustard on her own homemade bread. She pan-fried the ham, which was not processed. She didn't believe in processed products or "store-bought" bread, as her mom always called it. Also processed.

She placed the sandwich and a glass of whole milk on a table beside her recliner. She knew that as soon as she sat down in the recliner and put her feet up, almost before she could lay a blanket across her legs, her cat would jump up there to settle down for the evening.

She was a cat person.

The cat always "kneaded" her legs for a few minutes before she made several turns and settled down.

Also, as part of her routine, she turned on the TV to the local news at 5:00 p.m.

She was about to take a bite of her sandwich when they led with their main story: the murder in Dutch Mills. She sat up as much as she could without disturbing the cat, which was sensitive to her every movement.

They had not found the killer of the pastor's wife and had no leads, as of their last report. They were simply clue-less and admitted it. Since there had been a major thunderstorm that night, into the early morning, all clues had been washed away.

She put the sandwich back on the plate and put the plate on the table. She relaxed back onto the recliner. She closed her eyes, not hearing any more of the news.

She remembered that she had turned south on Highway 59 out of Dutch Mills. It was raining so hard she had to drive slower than she had originally hoped, but still made good time. She'd turned right (you can't turn left) on South Arkansas Highway 244, to the west. The alternative was going straight ahead. To the left was a small hill, completely covered with kudzu and Arkansas scrub brush.

She'd passed the two houses on the right, the only two houses on this three-quarter mile stretch of South Arkansas Highway 244 to the Oklahoma line, where it became Oklahoma 59.

When she reached State Line Road, before entering Oklahoma, she turned around. Well, it was always called State Line Road for years and years, but had recently been renamed Dutch Mills South for 911 purposes. This was the dirt, rocky road that came out of Dutch Mills to the south. By the time it hit Highway 244, it was just a few feet from the state line.

She'd stopped where the road met the highway, off the highway. She turned the car around to face east. It wouldn't pay for a vehicle to come too fast through this storm and run into her. She left the headlights on and turned on the emergency flashers. That should warn anyone she was sitting there.

Although she doubted anyone would make a connection with anything, she really did not want anyone to see the car here.

She reached into the backseat and brought up a black plastic bag. This bag contained a change of clothes, including socks and another pair of shoes.

She'd scooted her seat back as far as she could and started taking off the slicker and clothes beneath. Everything she had on, including underwear, came off. She stuffed them into another black plastic bag and dressed in the change of clothes as quickly as she could. Turning around and heading back the way she'd come was easy for her. After all, she had been traveling on that road, both directions, east and west, for around thirty-eight years now. She knew this short stretch like the back of her hand.

Confident that all was secured in the plastic bag, she moved onto the highway going east.

As she neared the driveway of the house on the left, the second driveway on the right as she approached, she pulled over by the large trash can sitting by the driveway entrance.

Although it was still raining "cats and dogs," she picked up the black, plastic trash bag from the passenger seat beside her, opened her door. She jumped out as quickly as she could, which she would have done even if it had not been raining, lifted the lid of the trash can. She quickly stuffed the plastic bag in the trash can, which made it about three-quarters full. She made sure the lid was firmly in place, so as not to come off with the rain and wind.

She just as quickly got back into the car and drove forward. In a few feet, she made a small dogleg left, a slight curve in the highway that put her out of sight of the next house or the house across a field, across the highway.

She knew the schedule. The rural trash service here would empty that trash can about 7:30 this morning. The people who lived here would pay no attention to the noise of the truck, since it was routine. By mid-morning the trash would be tossed onto the heap of refuse that made up the Stilwell, Oklahoma, landfill, which was located about fifteen miles south of town.

She'd proceeded to Arkansas Highway 59 and turned left (you can't go straight) toward home.

In the plastic bag were a black ski mask, full face, a black tee-shirt, black jacket, black pants, soft, fine black leather gloves, black socks and black shoes, underwear.

By this time, about four months later, give or take, the bag should be under at least fifty feet of other trash and dirt that was graded into the landfill by a front loader. The personnel at the landfill were very diligent about smoothing over the trash with the dirt they scooped out of each place the trash went.

This bag belonged among the rotting veggies, soiled papers, disposable diapers, meat bones from Sunday's pot roast and other rotting material. It would never be found.

During the last four months, her friend had definitely calmed down, whereas for at least a year before that, she was going to a therapist for her nerves, totally stressed out. She was no longer seeing a therapist.

Two months ago the little church at Dutch Mills had hired an interim, part-time music director until they could find someone willing to take the position full-time. Pastor Jennings just couldn't stay there any longer, so near to where his wife had been murdered. He moved to Florida to be closer to his family, as well as Maureen's.

The church had not started the process of locating a new pastor

The young man hired as interim music director was a student at John Brown University, which was located at Siloam Springs, about thirty miles to the north of Dutch Mills on the same Arkansas Highway 59. He came for an early choir practice on Sunday mornings, spent the afternoon if he needed to rest, in the parsonage, which had been cleared as a crime scene.

The young music director never went into the master bedroom, though, instead maybe taking a nap in one of the other bedrooms or watching TV to relax. Sometimes there were extra church activities during the day which he participated in.

He also drove down for Wednesday night services, when the choir practiced for Sunday, or other times. Right now, the choir was starting to practice for the Christmas cantata.

She smiled. They had an excellent organist.

Fortunately, this young man recognized good piano and organ playing when he heard it. He recognized talent, at any age. Instead of complaining about timing or tempo or "musical breaths," he complimented both ladies on their playing and thanked them after every practice and service.

Yes, definitely her friend was no longer stressed out, not so uptight she could hardly do her daily chores.

The one thing she could not bear to put in the plastic trash bag was the .22-caliber pistol with its extra ammo. This was not a new pistol. It had been her mother's pistol, one her mom had kept by her bed for at least thirty years, maybe even longer than that. Her mom kept it close for protection. She had lived by herself for many years after her husband left her, then her daughter and son-in-law had been with her for a year before her death several years before.

She made sure she took it when she went through her mother's things. She was the first to the house with a key. Her brother-in-law mentioned it a few days later, but she pretended she knew nothing about it. There had been so many people coming and going in the house between the time of her mom's death and the funeral.

Not being a new gun, bought before anyone had to register a gun purchase, there was no record of it anywhere. The ammo for it was still available, certainly at the Stilwell Walmart. Walmart recognized that people in that area simply did not buy new guns very often. There was no telling how many guns around there were years old.

She spent that first two months chipping out a hole the size of the gun out of the concrete foundation under the dryer. She had bought new grout and put the chips inside the hole around the gun, then re-grouted the tile in place.

One thing that had nagged at her for the last two months, however, was the fact that you could see about two inches of two squares of the tiles across the front of the dryer. The color of the new grout was a little off from the color of the old grout. If a person looked hard enough, you could tell there had been a replacement/repair job done under the dryer.

That bothered her.

She thought off and on to go buy new tiles and grout and replace the whole laundry room area. She wouldn't need more than sixteen tiles. She could do it, she had just always forgotten about it as soon as she thought of it. This time she wouldn't forget. It was that important.

Tomorrow.

Tomorrow morning, she would go to Lowe's at Springdale, buy the tiles and grout and replace it all. That way, the tile would all match and the gun would never be found.

She may never get to it again, but she didn't plan on moving from here, and she would know it was there.

Her mother's gun.

It had been her mother's gun for protection for so long.

She had so many memories of this gun.

And, after all, she herself had used this gun many times in the past for target practice.

She was sure it would never be found.

She sat back down in her recliner and picked up her sandwich, took a bite.

Nosirree, Bob.

No one could stress out her friend like that and get away with it.

⁊⁊⁊

The doorbell rang.

END

About the Author

Mary Jane Bryan is a graduate of Missouri State University (SEMO), Cape Girardeau, Missouri, with a B.S. in Business Administration/General Management and a graduate of Three Rivers Community College, Poplar Bluff, Missouri, with an A.A. in General Studies.

Bryan is a strong believer in women as entrepreneurs and managers, and a past creator and owner of Jane's Muppets. She is past member of Toastmasters International, which is an excellent resource for creative writing and presentation, receiving critiques and advice as needed. A past resident of Ecuador, Bryan now currently resides in Farmington, Missouri, with her husband, Peter, and their cat, Cookie.

9 781644 372821